Lonely in Happy Town

Praise for *Lonely in Happy Town*

"*Lonely in Happy Town* is a cozy but cathartic read about love, anxiety, and rebuilding community in the wake of COVID-19. Quentin's struggles with anxiety are nuanced and relatable, and love interest Celeste is sure to capture any reader's heart."

— E.M. Anderson, author of
The Remarkable Retirement of Edna Fisher

"[A] cozy mobile and console game offers the backdrop to a budding romance where queer teen Quentin, who finds life easier to live on the other end of a keyboard, crushes on two women, but one of them he only knows digitally. Social anxiety, finding your own bravery, and fighting for your own self-worth all become personal quests Quentin needs to master — if he can face them.

— 'Nathan Burgoine, author of
Stuck With You and *Dogs Don't Break Hearts*

"I was hooked on *Lonely in Happy Town* from Chapter 1. Kristopher Mielke has a talent for melding awkward teenager experiences with humour and heart."

— Jen Desmarais, author of
Crushing It and *Winging It*

Praise for *Losing Hit Points* by Kristopher Mielke

"The strength of *Losing Hit Points* is in its character reflections and celebration of queer joy. Journey is a flawed character who admits their flaws and becomes better because of it while allowing the reader to better understand one person's exploration of their gender identity. The host of side characters are all wonderful additions to the plot and bring their own essences and unique personalities . . . *Losing Hit Points* is a fun read with important conversations about identity and acceptance. Recommended."

— *CM: Canadian Review of Materials*

"This accessibly written title will draw in reluctant readers and appeal especially to gamers. Journey and their friends come across as true-to-life nerds . . . Will engage readers, leaving them alternately cheering and screaming at the cast."

— *Kirkus Reviews*

"Losing Hit Points is delightfully queer, wonderfully geeky, and brimming with heart—not to mention a fantastic introduction to Dungeons and Dragons for all ages."

— Darian Rudderham, Game Master, *Djinn & Tonics* podcast

Lonely in Happy Town

KRISTOPHER MIELKE

JAMES LORIMER & COMPANY LTD., PUBLISHERS
TORONTO

Published in Canada in 2025. Published in the United States in 2025.

James Lorimer & Company Ltd., Publishers acknowledges funding support from the Ontario Arts Council (OAC), an agency of the Government of Ontario. We acknowledge the support of the Canada Council for the Arts. This project has been made possible in part by the Government of Canada and with the support of Ontario Creates.

Cover design: Tyler Cleroux
Cover image: Shutterstock

Library and Archives Canada Cataloguing in Publication

Title: Lonely in Happy Town / Kristopher Mielke.
Names: Mielke, Kristopher, author.
Series: RealLove.
Description: Series statement: Real love
Identifiers: Canadiana (print) 2024051145X | Canadiana (ebook) 20240511476 | ISBN 9781459420045 (hardcover) | ISBN 9781459420038 (softcover) | ISBN 9781459420052 (EPUB)
Subjects: LCGFT: Novels.
Classification: LCC PS8626.I355 L66 2025 | DDC jC813/.6—dc23

Published by:
James Lorimer & Company Ltd., Publishers
117 Peter Street, Suite 304
Toronto, ON, Canada
M5V 0M3
www.lorimer.ca

Distributed in Canada by:
Formac Lorimer Books
5502 Atlantic Street
Halifax, NS, Canada
B3H 1G4
www.formaclorimerbooks.ca

Distributed in the US by:
Lerner Publisher Services
241 1st Ave. N.
Minneapolis, MN, USA
55401
www.lernerbooks.com

Printed and bound in Canada.

To Joyousenne Black, beloved friend and fearless leader of The Coconut Ducks.

01 Flying Frogs and Singing Fish

IT'S THE FIRST REAL SNOWFALL, and I'm stuck at work using my staff discount to drink more than the medically recommended dose of energy drinks. The windows of the convenience store are foggy from the battling temperatures on either side of the glass, but I can still see huge snowflakes speeding to the pavement.

Celeste, also trapped in this minimum wage prison, stands on a wobbly folding chair. She loosens the knot on a sparkly red ribbon above the door, taking down a sprig of plastic mistletoe, and tucking the fake plant into her back pocket. From her hip pocket, she pulls out something small, green, and roughly the same size.

"Careful," I warn her, "I tried taking the Christmas stuff down yesterday. George got real mad."

"Don't you worry," Celeste says. "I'm Indiana Jonesing this."

"That didn't work out great for Indiana Jones," I say.

"Hush, you."

I hum the *Indiana Jones* theme song as, sticking out her tongue, she uses the mistletoe ribbon to tie a toy frog to a small model rocket.

Christmas was three days ago, but George, the manager of our Halt N Purcha$e franchise, had us put up Christmas decorations and play Christmas music literally the week of Halloween. A sad plastic wreath hangs on the door above an ad for our $1 Chili Dog Tuesdays. The canned goods aisle wears a silver garland. I've lost Whamageddon every day for sixty-three days and counting.

The mistletoe was the most depressing touch. At best, it's a sad reminder that I'm seventeen and have never dated anyone, and that my first and only kiss ended a friendship. At worst, it's a harassment complaint waiting to happen. I have no problem with Celeste burning this corporate-sponsored idea of festive spirit to the ground.

She steps down from the chair, puts her hands on her hips, and admires her work. "What do you think?"

"Don't you think George will notice that you put up . . . a rocket frog?"

"Oh, Quentin, my naive co-worker. I put up *missile toad.*"

She smiles, huge and proud and goofy. I force myself to look at my hands before I stare at her for too long. "Are toads even green?"

"First of all, they can be. And second, these guys came from the dollar store. I think their quality leaves it up to interpretation."

"Do you still have to kiss under them?" I ask.

"Their function remains the same, yes. By law,

one must smooch. So watch out."

She puckers her lips and kisses in my direction.

The thing about my body is that it can't tell the difference between fantasy and reality. Sometimes the fantasy is a nightmare, which means I'll have a panic attack over a memory from third grade — crying at Steph Baxter's pool party is a regular rerun.

Other times, this time, the fantasy is clearly a joke. There is no possible reality in which Celeste Eguchi kissing me could happen.

But she's stopped in front of me, bracelets jingling as she leans with her tawny brown forearms on the counter.

Her lips glisten in the fluorescent lights, her lipstick the same colour as her dyed green pixie cut. I smell mint on her breath. Poking her tongue through her gum, she blows a bubble. It pops on her lips.

Her dark eyes lock onto mine for several moments too many.

I huff a laugh through my nostrils, adjusting my round glasses just for something to do with my hands.

With my whole face on fire, I say as little as I can get away with. "Noted."

She winks and pushes back from the counter. Moving the display stand of lighters an inch to the left, I take a deep breath as slowly and quietly as I can.

I'm used to being asked out as a joke. Like, "Ha ha, isn't the idea of *me* dating *you* funny?" But I don't think Celeste means it to sting quite as much as Steph did in third grade.

Thankfully, a customer interrupts my brewing thought spiral. A very thin man in a very large coat tosses a bag of sunflower seeds and a cheap lighter onto the counter. "Camels," he says, pointing to the stash of cigarettes behind me.

"Sure thing, Dave," Celeste says, grabbing the smokes.

I ring him through. He returns to the blizzard from whence he came, never to know how thankful I am that he reset the Halt N Purcha$e vibe.

Celeste pops another stick of gum into her mouth. She adds a new piece every time someone buys cigarettes. The habit started with nicotine gum, but she switched to spearmint a couple months ago.

I sip my lukewarm coffee energy drink. Perched on the stool next to me, Celeste has gone back to silently swiping on her phone screen. Probably texting a boyfriend who, in my imagination, is unreasonably tall and British and drives a motorcycle.

Our interactions usually come in waves — with my head underwater, my lungs filling with my own anxiety.

"You can take your break early," I offer.

She swings an arm, gesturing to the empty store without looking up. "Can you handle our booming business all on your own?"

"I'll survive somehow."

"This is why you're my favourite. Bee-are-bee."

I stare at the clear plastic counter and the rainbow of lottery tickets, letting my brown, overgrown bangs fall in front of my face. A built-in shield for avoiding eye contact. Celeste heads to the back room.

I haven't seen her smoke since April. The day

before she told me to call her Celeste, and to use she/her pronouns, or *face her wrath*. The announcement was sudden and intense, like she expected some backlash from me, but I know how anxiety can be. Especially anxiety around coming out.

At the time, I didn't know how seriously to take the follow-up announcement that she was quitting cigarettes. She took a *lot* of smoke breaks, and I always saw her in the big group of smokers by the creek at school. But she wanted to "become the best possible Celeste."

I'm proud of her . . . but I would never say it. We don't have that kind of relationship. Er, friendship, I mean. Co-worker dynamic.

Celeste bursts from the break room in full winter gear like she's trekking the Arctic — her long fur-lined jean coat, a black toque, and the thickest mittens I've ever seen. She waves at me before heading out into the cold.

The chill hasn't even left the air before I take out my phone and open the *Happy Town* app.

Little cutesy animal faces dot the loading screen. It takes longer on my mobile data because Halt N Purcha$e is way too cheap for good wi-fi, even though there are at least five of them in Kitchener alone. The mobile version of *Happy Town* has way fewer features than the desktop version, too. But I'm only checking one thing.

Please be online tonight.

The thought grips my racing heart and doesn't let go, a crushing hand wrapped around the pathetic little songbird in my chest.

Finally, the game loads. My avatar wakes up. I play a salt-and-pepper-coloured hedgehog, living in a home I haven't redecorated since the big Halloween event . . . two years ago.

Harry the Hedgehog sits up in his coffin, dressed in a Winnie-the-Pooh-style cap and nightgown. He yawns, stretches his little arms, and hops to the floor. Quickly changing into a black hoodie, Harry runs downstairs to a living room furnished with jack-o'-lanterns, cobwebs, and skeletons. He steps out the front door.

The virtual suburbs are fully holiday themed, with colourful Christmas lights wrapped around the trees and snow falling from the sky. Neighbours in ugly Christmas sweaters and Santa outfits run around, talking to NPCs and doing their little side quests.

It's like real life, only less depressing.

Above the mailbox at the end of the lawn is an icon of an envelope, with a little wrapped gift attached. Harry opens the mailbox. The letter expands to fit the screen:

> *Dear Harry the Hedgehog,*
>
> *It is with a heavy heart that I must inform you of my massive wealth. I simply have too much cash for one girl to avoid spending. With this in mind, I have purchased for you the fanciest gift. Please gaze upon it daily and think of how cool I am.*
>
> *Sincerely,*
> *Mabel*

If snow landed on my face right now, it'd sizzle. Mabel has a habit of putting a match to my head and letting me go up in flames.

With a tap, I direct my avatar to open the gift. The bow unties and the lid lifts. A little rewarding jingle plays as Harry holds the gift above his head. It's a fish.

The fish wiggles and sings, "*Never gonna give you up–*"

I burst out laughing.

The store bell chimes as Celeste comes back inside, covered in snow. She wipes her boots on the bloated front mat, each step squishing loudly. "What's so funny?"

"Oh, nothing," I say in a hurry, putting my phone in sleep mode. "Just playing a game."

"Slacking off? For shame, Q." Celeste unwinds her scarf and shrugs out of her coat. Her cheeks and the tip of her nose are rosy from the cold. "What game?"

I should probably lie, but I'm not quick enough on my feet. My brain feet. See?

"*Happy Town*," I mumble.

She smirks.

I overflow with dread like a Slurpee cup in the hands of a preteen. "It's just this kids' game. For dumb babies. You decorate your house, or, like, start a farm, or do quests and other stuff. It's, like, an everything game. And all the players are anthropomorphic animals. Like, animals that are people. I hate it, actually. It's the worst. Forget you ever saw me playing it."

A sample of the things I'd rather be doing than embarrassing myself in front of Celeste: homework, giving the cat a bath, brain surgery, the list goes on. At least I said "anthropomorphic" right on the first try.

"Uh-huh. I've heard of the game that literally everybody played at the beginning of the pandemic," she says, still smirking.

And that's the last we talk about it that night. The death knell of her respect for me.

The final hour of our shift passes in thick silence. I replay this disaster of a conversation in my head the whole time, my stomach tight and nauseated. There are no more customers. The snow keeps falling, piling high on the snowbanks, turning to slush in the street.

I should have lied and said I was playing something manly. Something with guns or race cars — go-karts don't count. A real video game for real Men.

We're not even one of the cool stores open twenty-four hours, unlike the ones on Ottawa Street or near the Charles Street bus terminal, so at 11 p.m. we lock up. The key freezes in my ungloved hand. Celeste bounces on the toes of her burgundy leather boots. Clouds of minty breath stream from her mouth.

She notices me looking at her. Snowflakes whisper as they hit the rising ground. The lock *thunk*s shut.

Celeste smiles. "See ya later, Q."

We walk in opposite directions. At the stop sign, I turn back to find she's already gone.

If only I didn't have to go home.

02 Octopus Stereotypes

WHEN I GET TO MY EMPTY HOME, I turn on all the lights, sit at my computer desk, and load up *Happy Town*. I turn up the volume and the chill, jazzy *Happy Town* theme music fills my bedroom. Sure, it's almost midnight, but I can't sleep without checking for Mabel.

As Harry steps outside, I scan my short Friend List. She's online. It says she's at the Marsupial Marketplace. Opening the World Map, I click on the marketplace, and Harry teleports.

So I lied about hating this baby game. Obviously. I've been obsessed since it came out when I was in grade six, six years ago. It's cute. It's cozy. The non-player characters love me unconditionally — unless I give them a bad gift, like a stick, or expired milk.

And the player characters can be pretty great, too.

I find her immediately. A purple axolotl in an ugly Christmas sweater. The most embarrassing creature to have a crush on.

Snow continues to fall in-game and outside my window. My laptop fan roars, keeping plastic and zinc computer guts from melting all over my desk. Rover, my twenty-five-pound diabetic black cat, jumps onto my lap.

"Oof," I say.

A thought bubble appears over Mabel's head: a picture of a shining fish with rainbow scales. The Rainbow Fish — one of the rarest fish in the entire game. There's something like a 0.0001 percent chance of finding it. Selling one means she's caught more.

Player characters line up to trade. Rainbow Fish

are already worth more than most items in the game, but fishing in *Happy Town* is actual Hell. And also the December fishing tournament ends in a couple hours. Presenting the NPC judges with a Rainbow Fish is the only way to get the Proud Angler achievement.

Not an achievement I care about but like I said, *Happy Town* really is The Everything Game. Endless and constantly updated, with every mini-game imaginable. You can farm, play competitive cards, race go-karts, play a rhythm-game concert for an audience, or enter your home into competitions. It's the metaverse Mark Zuckerberg and other weird crypto guys wish they had.

Personally, I like to spend my time talking to NPCs, getting to know more about the characters. Oh, and shaking trees until money falls out.

An exclamation point appears over the head of Princess the Cat, an NPC known mostly for eating tuna sandwiches. Not the best example of a richly detailed character. Mabel's busy, so I make Harry accept the quest.

Princess:

Thanks, HARRY! I simply can't have my daily catnap without a **tuna fish sandwich**! Purr-haps you'll find **whole-grain bread** at **Maisel's Bakery**, *meow, meow*!

My phone rings, propped up against a worn copy of *King of Coats* on my desk. I swipe right. The screen fills with a big, brown eyeball.

"Hey, where you at?" says Ramy, my best — and only — friend.

He leans back, confirming that he is not, in fact, a giant floating eyeball. His long, curly black hair is even bigger than usual, probably due to the Florida humidity. His normally brown complexion is already darker from the week of coastal sun.

"Marsupial Market," I say.

"And whatcha doing there?" he says in a tone that makes me wish he were here so I could push him.

As my only friend, Ramy gets to know all my embarrassing secrets. It's hard enough having one crush and keeping it to yourself, the way crushes squirm in the belly like swallowing a live octopus. Unfortunately, Ramy can't be trusted.

"Leave me alone," I whine. "You fled the country. You don't get to call me out."

"Ah, yes, fleeing the country . . . to go on vacation with my family."

"Abandoning me."

"What was I supposed to say? 'No, Mom, I don't want to visit Auntie Iman's beachfront property. I think I'd rather stay in Canada during its wretched winter and play online video games with Quentin.' Doesn't sound very reasonable to me, buddy."

"You're online right now! Playing video games with me!"

As if I summoned him, a fox in a watermelon-patterned t-shirt and aviator sunglasses appears out of thin air beside Harry. His nickname tag, Reynard, floats above his head.

Reynard:

nuh-uh

Reynard runs in circles around Harry, then does squats.

"Besides the point," Ramy says. "I've got nothing else to do. Iman's pool is overflowing with iguanas. We're under an iguana advisory."

"At least it's not alligators," I say.

"Don't joke. I saw two gators on the road into town. They smiled at me and licked their lips."

"Alligators don't have lips."

Ramy waves away the criticism. "Says the guy not in Florida. How's it going in Not-Florida?"

I let out a breath it feels like I've been holding all week, and I spill my guts uncontrollably. The last week was a mess. We were invited to my uncle's farm for Christmas, but Dad's either been at work or asleep on the couch, and didn't feel like getting up come December 25, 2 p.m. Then Mom sent me a text that just said, "Merry Christmas!" from her new house in Leeds, the United Frickin' Kingdom, where she lives with her new boyfriend.

"You haven't seen anybody but your dad all week?

What about your favourite co-worker?" There's that tone again. I can *hear* his eyebrows waggling. "What's Celeste up to?"

I make Harry equip his axe and swing it at Reynard.

The blade passes through the fox harmlessly, but Ramy still says, "Hey!"

"Everyone with a job has a favourite co-worker," I say.

"Yeah, they're called your work wife. Would you prefer I say that?"

"I'd prefer you be nice to me. I can't help who I have a crush on, but it doesn't mean anything. We're just co-workers."

"That might be what the official Halt N Purcha$e paperwork says, but your heart says otherwise. I can hear it from all the way in my aunt's iguana-infested bungalow." Ramy rolls his office chair backward and cranes his neck, I guess to look out the window. "Seriously, they're having a pool party out there. One of them has a piña colada."

"You're a bully."

"Yeah, well, this bully's got to go. The guild's tackling the Stalking Stork and they'll lose it if I miss another raid. Everyone needs a healer, but no one respects one. I'm like the drummer of our band."

"Except with fewer real-life skills," I say.

"With a face this pretty, who needs skills?" Ramy folds his hands under his chin and smiles. When I refuse to validate him, he sticks out his tongue and resets. "Invitation's still open if you want in. You might be a little less lonely if you joined a guild."

He keeps trying to get me to join The League of Extraordinarily Gentle Hens. But I don't like the *World of Warcraft* culture bleeding into *Happy Town*. The last couple updates brought new mini-games and storylines catering to an audience that only wants to hit things.

"Guilds are boys' clubs," I say with disgust.

"May I remind you, you are a boy," Ramy says. "And you're bisexual."

"I am attracted to men reluctantly and without my consent."

"Imagine being so picky. I'd never be able to date."

"With the boyfriends you introduce to me? You could be a little pickier."

Ramy recoils from the webcam like he touched a hot stove. "Ouch! Harsh!"

"I regret nothing."

"That could be the last thing you ever say to me, Quentin. I could be eaten by a gator tomorrow."

"I'd say it again."

"*Wow*, okay," he says. "What would you do after my funeral? Finally make a move on your work wife? Or finally make a move on your *Happy Town* wife?"

"Don't you have to go?"

"Not until you change your avatar to a chicken."

"Hedgehogs are already armoured balls afraid of getting hurt," I say.

"Whose side are you on?" Ramy asks.

"The side of truth. Of justice."

"You must enjoy hopelessly pining all day."

"There's nothing wrong with pining. Romance novels are a bestselling genre."

"Whatever you say, lover boy. Catch you later."

Ramy ends the call. Reynard vanishes. The crowd around Mabel is starting to thin, with only the most serious potential buyers left.

I spin around in my busted office chair, my walls of memorabilia blurring. Old *Mario* and *Minecraft* posters on the walls. Manga and fantasy books sharing a bookshelf that's actually mostly video games. Hanging shelves lined with *Happy Town* Funko Pops, plushies, and toys with lots of posable joints that cost way too much. Relics from when I could afford to spend all my Halt N Purcha$e paycheque on fun stuff.

Finally, Mabel stands alone in the market square. Despite all the pining, a hedgehog is hardly the hero of a romance novel, but I make Harry approach her.

Ellipses appear over Mabel's head. Her message appears in a chat box on the right side of my screen.

Mabel:

like the gift? :)

Mabel the Axolotl swings her arms and dances

a little. Maybe behind the screen, the real Mabel is smiling, too. I blush, alone in my room. Rover vibrates like a power tool, crushing my thighs.

I type a reply.

Harry:

no one's ever rick roll'd me so masterfully

Mabel:

i suspected not

but i'm no amateur

i went to the Academy of Rick Rolling

I open the Actions Wheel and click Laugh. Harry the Hedgehog leans back in laughter, holding his belly. Tears fly from his eyes. The animation times out and, abruptly, he stops.

Harry:

it's a privilege to be pranked by the best

how are things?

We haven't talked in a couple days, because she's probably a normal person who sees family over the holiday. She says she's dreading exams next month. I tell her all the ways my Christmas sucked. We're kindred spirits on a children's game, complaining about the lives we're powerless to change.

It's different than with Ramy. Mabel doesn't judge.

Other players run around and between us, holding flowers, butterfly nets, wrenches, other assorted items. Uncaring that we're having a moment here. More thought bubbles show players selling frog-shaped chairs and enchanted hats.

Mabel:

wanna relocate?

In my inbox, an invite appears to a private server in the location where we met: The Octopus's Garden. Our spot.

The axolotl vanishes. I accept the invitation. My

screen goes black except for the loading bar.

(I read somewhere that loading bars don't really mean anything. A placebo for impatient video game players used to instant gratification. It feels like a punishment.)

Mabel sits on a bench overlooking the ocean. On an island in the middle distance, a full crustacean band jams. The digital sunset fills the sky with a rainbow of colour. It always looks like that, a place untouched by time.

I make Harry sit next to her.

Harry:

it's unfair they always make the octopus a drummer

what if he wanted an 8-necked guitar

Mabel:

he should follow his 3 hearts

i believe in him.

Then we just sit in comfortable silence. Through

my speakers, the waves crash into the surf. Calm music plays, the melodic smacking of octopus arms against a steel drum.

Crushes are like a virus. You can't use antibiotics. There is no cure. You just have to wait it out. Either you get better or . . . you die, I guess?

And yeah, I've been to an anti-internet propaganda assembly. I've had forty-year-old men with way too much energy jump around on stage and tell me how not to get human trafficked. What if Mabel's a pervert trying to catfish me — or worse yet, what if she's married?

Obviously, I've wondered. I have a lot of anxiety. I've asked if we can add each other on real social media. If she wants to text. She said no. That it's a safety issue for her. So we agreed to stay internet friends and never share any real information. No real locations, besides Southern Ontario generally. No real names.

I'm obsessed with a girl whose face I can't even picture. That makes it hard to fantasize about her without picturing an axolotl. Not impossible, as I've looked up the cost of bus and train rides across the province, wondering which city she might be in. I've imagined a hundred different faces, wearing a hundred different expressions the moment she finally meets me. Would she be happy? Nervous? Disappointed? Probably disappointed . . .

The bigger problem is, Ramy is annoying — and not wrong to point out how hopeless I am. I have a crush on two different girls, neither of whom will ever reciprocate those feelings.

03 Skanking, Fig Newtons, and Other Mysteries

THROUGH THE BIG STOREFRONT WINDOW, I see Celeste kicking her legs and flailing her arms. I think she's dancing? I kick my boots against the brick wall, knocking off the snow.

When I open the front door, music overwhelms me, upbeat guitars thrashing and brassy horns blaring. Celeste sees me but keeps dancing. More aggressively, if anything. She looks like a floppy, noodle-armed 1930s cartoon character going for a walk.

"What are you doing?" I shout over a trombone solo. The temperature change fogs over the lenses of my glasses, but I can still hear her panting, her shoes scuffing the floor.

"Sorry!" Celeste cries breathlessly. "Can't talk! Skanking!"

"*What*?"

Half-blind, I hang my coat up in the back room and take my place behind the counter. I wipe my glasses on the hem of my black Halt N Purcha$e polo. Celeste is completely bent over, still swinging and kicking. A braver person would jump in and join her, but I've never figured out how to dance without feeling like the world's biggest idiot.

The song ends, and in the sudden silence, Celeste's sneakers squeak loudly on the linoleum. She stops, taking off her black toque and sweeping back her sweaty green bangs.

Celeste fills her rosy cheeks with air and puffs out

a breath. "Sorry you had to see that, Q. When We Are the Union comes on, the skanking takes over. Such is the power of ska."

I can feel myself making a face. "Ska? Like the mozzarella sticks meme?"

"Oh my god, Q, that is so offensive."

I can't tell if she's joking. Genuinely, everything I know about ska is from one picture I've seen on the internet of a bunch of guys with trombones that says, "Ska is what plays in a kid's head when he gets mozzarella sticks." I have never voluntarily listened to ska but after what I just heard, the meme hasn't been disproven.

"Isn't ska dead?" I ask. "Did ska ever really live?"

"So uncultured. You have no idea how gay and cool new ska is."

She pulls her phone out of her pocket, and I catch a flash of her background photo — her and some tall, handsome guy, their arms around each other's shoulders. He's East Asian like her, though I obviously can't tell if he's also Japanese. His eyes pierce into my soul. His sharp jaw could defeat mine in combat.

Then Spotify opens. Celeste's Bluetooth speaker plays the opening of a song with jumpy, halting electric guitar and the singer addressing an apparently hostile audience.

"Really listen to the lyrics," she says, leaning close with spearmint on her breath. "It's an anthem about queer joy. About fighting back against small-minded pricks."

Horns and drums join the guitar, and the beat takes off. It's not subtle, and that's a good thing. It's loud. It's joyous. It is, actually, incredible. Celeste watches me, gauging my reaction, and I realize I'm bobbing my head.

When the song ends, I say, "I see the error of my ways."

Her hand lands on my back. My stomach twists up like a Twizzler.

"Like all prejudice, ska-phobia is taught in our oppressive culture," she says. "It's not your fault. But you can be better."

I snort a laugh. She turns on another song and

dances away. I busy myself stocking the shelves.

We're not the cool kind of convenience store where you can still buy obscure flavours of Coke and imported candy, like Japanese Kit-Kats in flavours only Willy Wonka could approve. We're the global chain that pops up like weeds and strangles places like that to death. We sell Fig Newtons even though nobody buys them, which is probably because no one knows what a "newton" is, and who even eats figs? Wasps die in figs!

Celeste's checking the temperature on the rotating hot dog cooker when we get our first customer of the day. He ties his dog to a Reserved Parking sign and tracks in big clumps of snow with him.

"Hey, Mickey," Celeste says.

The old man grunts in response and continues to the beef jerky aisle.

Celeste laughs. The sound makes my chest warm.

She's a thousand times friendlier than me. I've been working here for a year and a half and I still never really know what to do when customers are shopping.

I hate when I'm shopping and an employee asks me if I need help. Even if I do need help.

"You're coming by Thursday, right?" Celeste asks, grabbing the clipboard under the counter and logging the temp.

I almost think she's talking to me, but Mickey grunts again.

"Oh, you love my soup, don't even pretend," she says. "My chicken noodle could win awards."

Mickey tosses jerky, margarine, a loaf of bread, and a carton of buttermilk onto the counter. At his request, I add a scratch ticket, and ring him through.

As he leaves, Celeste shouts, "Thursday!"

"Uh-huh."

Why is Celeste inviting a strange old man to dinner?

When the door shuts behind him, she catches the expression on my face and bursts out laughing. "I'm sure I don't want to know what you're thinking."

"Probably not," I say.

"It's dinner at a soup kitchen, not my house. I

volunteer at The Souper Centre at least once a month. More on the holidays, they're extra hard for a lot of people."

"That's awesome. Volunteering is, I mean. Not holidays being extra hard . . ."

I cringe. What an understatement. I say "awesome" for so many things that do not inspire actual *awe* that I sound like a dick now even though I mean it. A teenage girl volunteers hours of her life to give people free food! The most charitable thing I do is . . . um . . .

"So you actually do know them," I say, changing the subject.

"Who, Mickey?" Celeste asks.

"Yeah. And Dave. And, you know, everybody. You're always referring to customers by name."

"Is that weird?"

"I always wondered if you were making them up," I say.

"Q!" Celeste gasps, placing a hand against her chest. "I'm wounded. You think I would refer to somebody by a name they did not give me? I'll have you know,

Stoner Dave is one of my favourite customers."

"I still can't tell if you're joking."

"No way. He works at the Fischer-Hallman Wendy's and sometimes gives me free fries. Before you got here, I saw Fred, who sells weed to Stoner Dave behind the dumpster on Tuesdays. Oh, and Sheila, the middle-aged redhead who looks like she'd kill for just one night of babysitting for the twins, Jolene and Andy. The kids who run down the aisles and touch all the candy."

"How?" I say, still genuinely in awe.

"I . . . pay attention? And ask? I grew up in a small town. Knowing your neighbours comes naturally." She shrugs. "I don't know, man. I'm a friendly person."

"Does not compute," I say. "If it were that easy, I'd have friends by now."

I need to shut up. There's no sadder, more attention-begging sentence than "boo hoo, I have no friends." They shouldn't let me leave the house.

"Come on, you have friends," Celeste says, because I have forced her into having to make me feel better.

"You're always hanging out with Ramy at school."

Before I can think better of it, I say, "You notice me at school?"

"Uh, yeah. We work together, dude. Of course I notice you. In school. At the mall. At the bus stop. We've known each other since I moved to Kitchener."

"Oh. You never say hi."

Celeste's playful grin fades, her dark eyebrows rising in surprise. For probably the first time, she seems like the one caught off guard. "I do so. Like, all the time. You always ignore me, staring straight ahead, looking a little like someone ran over your cat."

"I'm pretty sure Rover would cause damage to their car." I point at my face with both hands and frown deeper than anyone but a mime should. "Sorry some of us have resting grumpy face."

Celeste blows a raspberry as a laugh forces its way out of her. "You don't have to apologize for your face."

"You say that but I don't feel it. Anyway, yeah, that sounds like me in literally any social situation. I probably thought you were talking to someone else."

"I just figured you were one of those guys who doesn't do anything work related on their time off. Now I know Quentin is open to greetings in non-work settings. Maybe even small talk."

"Let's not get ahead of ourselves." I say it with a straight face I've been practicing as long as I've developed a sense of humour. Mom said I was British in a past life, before I knew that was foreshadowing. Celeste looks like she's taking me seriously, so I say, "Kidding."

She leans on the counter, lacing fingers painted with shiny chrome nail polish. "So, what have you and Ramy been up to over break?"

"He left for Florida the Thursday before break even started."

"Oh. What have you been up to over break, then?"

"Working," I say.

"Gripping stuff." Celeste grins, proving I am exactly as embarrassing as I fear. She sits up straight and turns to face me. "Pretend Ramy's here. What would you be doing tonight?"

I turn toward the window. To the winter wonderland that showed up out of nowhere yesterday. "If I wasn't working until 11 p.m.? Probably tobogganing down Mt. Trashmore."

"I love tobogganing! Let's do it."

I blink at her. "Together?"

"Unless you'd rather go alone?" she says. "You can tell me if I'm coming on too strong — I've been told I can't tell when people don't want to hang out with me. A side effect of being this friendly, probably."

Panic shakes me by the shoulders, slaps me out of my stupor. Celeste wants to hang out. With *me*. And I'm majorly screwing it up.

"No, I'd love to," I say. Wait, dammit, *love* is such a big word. *Walk it back.* "I mean, I'd enjoy–enjoy hanging out. A normal amount."

Celeste purses her lips and narrows her eyes, in an obvious attempt not to laugh at me yet again. "Can't wait."

04 The Summit of Trash Mountain

STOPPING OUTSIDE MY HOUSE, I see the worst thing possible: the car in the driveway. This means not only is Celeste seeing my place for the first time, but she'll also *meet my dad*.

I flash back to the outfit he's been wearing around the house. A stained, ripped t-shirt. Heart boxers. *Grey socks*. No, I can't subject either of them to the trauma of an introduction under these circumstances.

"What's up?" Celeste asks. We've been standing

in the middle of my front lawn while I make these calculations. "You do live here, right?"

"Uh. Yeah. Can you wait here?" I ask.

"No worries," she says.

I run up my front steps, slipping inside. Annoyingly, my glasses fog up again, trying their best to become useless.

Giving the lenses a wipe and kneeling before the hall closet, I realize way too late how rude it is to make Celeste wait in the cold. Not rude enough to make me change my mind, but it is the kind of memory I'll probably replay later. The kind that makes my soul shrivel up in shame, that causes hyperventilation and panic attacks. I'm cursed by the self-awareness to know every choice I make will be the wrong one until I die.

"Quentin?" Dad calls.

I grab my green plastic toboggan from the hall closet before leaning in view of the living room. "Hey. Didn't think you'd be home."

Dad's on the couch with a beer bottle. He's dressed more or less in exactly the outfit I feared, brown hair shaggy and beard having forgotten what a razor even looks like. Alex Trebek's voice plays from the TV. Dad watches nothing but old *Jeopardy* episodes on Netflix these days.

"My back's acting up," he says.

"Did you take pain meds?" I ask.

He waves his beer, liquid sloshing against the bottle's walls. "Got all the pain management I need."

I sigh and head to the bathroom. He can't take medication while drinking, but I grab the heating pad from where it hangs on the towel rack. Dropping the toboggan on the carpet, I lean over Dad to plug the heating pad in behind the couch. He cranes his neck to see the TV.

"You didn't have to," he grumbles.

"Too late," I say. "You're welcome."

He wriggles the heating pad behind him, wrapping it around his middle.

"God, it's like I'm your dad," I say as I secure the Velcro.

Brow furrowed behind his large glasses, Dad's gaze

remains on the television. "What do you mean by that?"

"Don't worry about it." I pick up the toboggan.

Behind my dad, the burgundy wall is long and empty. There's a missing piece, an absence where for my entire childhood there had been one of my mom's paintings.

My parents were a pandemic breakup. Two people who realized they didn't actually like each other that much once they were forced to stay in the same house all the time. Too often, they forgot we were actually three people trapped in the same house.

Within these thin walls, it's just me and my father. But three steps backward, and I'm free — free from the stale air and stifling sadness. Free from memories of Mom. Free from expecting Dad to care whether or not I break my neck on Mt. Trashmore in the middle of the night.

My knuckles ache around the toboggan's handle. My neck flushes, itchy and hot. My heart beats too fast, an engine fueled by anger. "I'm heading out."

"Okay."

My parents used to make me text them updates when I was out of the house. Changes of address, who I was hanging out with, what time to expect me home. It was super annoying. But at least they gave a shit.

I throw open the front door, grateful for the cold on my overheating cheeks. The door closes behind me. I take a deep breath.

Celeste is gone.

She's right to leave. I don't deserve to have friends. I don't need anyone else seeing this sad picture. I'm such a loser I can't even . . .

There are two sets of footprints in the snow. The first are mine, leading from where we first stood on the lawn to where I stand now. The second lead under the awning that covers the car, and to the back gate. Metal clinks faintly from the backyard.

I catch my breath and follow Celeste's footsteps. My free-standing hammock swings gently. Celeste lies in it with her hands behind her head.

"Sorry," she says, "got bored. This is a sweet setup. Must be great in the summer."

I haven't used it in years. Not since —

Max's body pressed tight to mine, both of us gathered in the middle of the hammock, talking about the sky, and stars, and other worlds —

"I guess so," I say.

She swings her legs out of the hammock and sits up. "Ready to go?"

***

When I was really little, Mt. Trashmore was just a great big hill in a great big field, surrounded by dirt trails with a couple of ponds in their ditches. Before that, in the '70s, it was a humongous trash pile, a garbage dump too close to future suburban culs-de-sac. After people moved in, they had to evacuate because the methane gas in the area was dangerous.

I guess it's fine now because they renamed it McLennan Park and installed an expensive playground, a splash pad, and a dog park. Everyone still calls it Mt. Trashmore, though.

The park is mostly empty, except for a group of

people I think I know from school, passing around a bottle of Goldschläger. The bits of gold sparkle in the street light.

I look at my soaked running shoes, my freezing toes, and focus on the scrape of the toboggan behind me.

But Celeste raises a hand and says, "Hey, Steph!"

"Celeste!" replies a feminine voice I definitely know. "And . . . Quentin Evans, is that you?"

I look up to meet the surprised green eyes of Steph Baxter. She of relived birthday party flashback fame. The girl who, on more than one occasion, asked me on a date as a joke, tried to pants me (but couldn't because I happened to be wearing a belt), and spread the rumour that I was in love with Kelsey Hale in the grade above ours. Sure, it was true, but Steph wasn't exactly trying to be my wingman.

These days she's in my calc class. She hasn't spoken to me — or about me — since high school began. Her long blonde hair, contoured cheeks, and hourglass figure in her leather jacket are all immediately intimidating.

Her friends today aren't her usual crowd. I'm pretty sure I know them from the times I've hovered at the door to the Gay-Straight Alliance before chickening out. A short guy with a gold septum ring and pink buzz cut nods at me.

"Uh, yeah. Hi." I wave with one hand and put my other in my pants pocket, pushing down just enough to feel the resistance of my belt on my hips. Better safe than sorry.

"How's your sister?" Celeste asks.

She fully stops walking. I have no choice but to wait for her, though every atom in my body begs me to run away.

"She wishes she left Kitchener earlier," Steph says. "Hard not to take it personally, but at least she's happy. She loves it in Toronto."

"Good for her."

Steph extends the bottle of Goldschläger. "You guys want some? There's plenty to go around."

I eye the sloshing transparent alcohol with no enthusiasm. I've tried a couple drinks at family functions. Tried a couple more with Ramy, though drinking is haram — his reasoning being, "If I'm going to avoid sin, I should know what the sin is like." It made sense for me, too.

Alcohol always makes me impulsive and, like, ten times sadder. Thinking about becoming somebody excited about drinking makes it a thousand times sadder.

Thankfully, Celeste says, "Nah, we're going to need our faculties. No drunk driving this toboggan. You folks have fun, though."

She leads us away from the company and the only source of light, save for the nearly full moon and cloudless sky turning the blanket of deep white into a luminous force.

When we're out of earshot, I say, "You're still doing it."

"What's that?" she asks.

"Talking to everyone. Knowing everyone. How do I fix my resting grumpy face?"

"I could tell you to just fake it 'til you make it, but I'm sure you've been told that."

"Endlessly." I shake my head. "And I have tried. I know, as an adult, I'll have to do hard things sometimes. It's just . . . I keep waiting for it to get easier. Less scary. It hasn't."

"Exactly. Not everyone can force themselves to be, I don't know, neurotypical? Maybe you have social anxiety. Maybe you're autistic. Maybe there's too much pressure to conform in life, just generally. Give yourself a break."

I've gotten a lot of criticism for my anxiety. For having a hard time ordering at restaurants, or thanking family for Christmas presents, or presenting in class. Just thinking about being called up by the teacher makes my hands shake, my heart beat relentlessly, and my mind plan a hasty exit.

Not once has anyone told me it's *okay*. That being anxious doesn't mean being a failure.

We leave the trail and begin the climb.

05 Trauma Dump at the Former Dumpsite

TRUDGING UP THE STEEP HILL, we slip on the icy, well-worn paths and the foot of fresh snow. Mt. Trashmore is *tall*. I don't know exactly how tall, but it takes at least five breathless minutes to climb in the summer, and right now it is *not* summer.

The snow slides loose under my feet. I fall, hitting the hill, and slide backward. Down, and down, and down — until I jam a hand into the hillside.

"You good?" Celeste calls from above.

"Could be worse," I say, brushing the snow from my stinging fingers. I hold up the rope of the toboggan still gripped in my other hand. "Almost let go."

Kicking my feet into the snow for better support, like I'm wearing those ice-climbing shoes with the little picks, I slowly catch up to Celeste. The climb begins again. I'm so out of breath by the time we reach the summit, I can't speak.

We haven't even gone downhill and my pants and shoes are already soaked. My winter coat hangs open as if to invite the bitter wind, its zipper teeth chipped away. Replacing winter gear takes money I don't have. Every paycheque since Mom left has gone toward groceries . . . and paying my *Happy Town* subscription, but that's a mental health expense.

At the top of the hill, you can see for miles — sorry to the rest of Canada, but *kilometres* just isn't as satisfying a word. Waves of twinkling suburbia and swaths of dark forest turn into tall apartment buildings, and cranes building more, taller apartment buildings. I can see my whole neighbourhood.

I take a deep breath of frozen air. Exhale a cloud of condensation. Rub my hands together, knuckles dry beneath my fingertips. With the light of Kitchener on all sides, nostalgia settles into my gut. Things used to be better. Even when they were hard, they didn't seem *this* hard.

A stick of lip chap floats in front of my face.

Celeste presses her lips together. "Want some?"

I stare at the lip chap. The chap that has touched her lips. "Are you sure?"

"Yeah, why not?"

I swallow with a mouth suddenly much too dry. Mumbling my thanks, I take the lip chap. Uncap it. Apply the flat cylinder of balm to my own lips, praying Celeste can't tell how badly I'm blushing.

To get my mind off of how awkward I'm making *everything*, I say, "I've been coming up here basically forever."

"Yeah?" Celeste asks, taking the lip chap from me. "Were you born in Kitchener?"

"At Grand River Hospital. Lived in my house my whole life. Been doing the same routine until . . ." I stop myself from talking about last year. It's depressing enough for one person. "Anyway, I'm all about Kitchener stuff. Stuff like a shrine of Onkel Hans the Oktoberfest guy above our fireplace."

She giggles and says, "There's no way."

"He's a local hero. What about you?"

"I am not a local hero."

"That's what every true hero would say. You literally volunteer in the local area." I pause, expecting a back-and-forth, but she says nothing. "But I mean, you weren't always a Kitchen . . . Kitchenette? Kitchenerite? You said you grew up in a small town."

"Bright," Celeste says.

"Never heard of it," I say.

"Not surprising. When I lived there, it barely had five hundred people. No hospital, no library, no school. Just old retirees, families, and kids passing the time until they can leave — or they realize they're trapped."

"I'm guessing you didn't like it much."

Celeste crosses her arms. “I think your hometown is kind of like a family member. Even if you hate them, even if you cut them out of your life, they’re a part of you. You are who you are because of them, a least a little. I don’t like Bright. But I kind of love Bright. You know?”

Nodding, I fix my gaze on home. I really do get it.

“It was not the ideal place to grow up queer, that’s for sure,” Celeste says. “Not a lot of patience for boys with long hair or a love of My Little Ponies, let alone boys who wear a dress when they think they’ll be home alone for a couple hours.”

“I wouldn’t say Kitchener is a gay paradise,” I say. “At least we have Tri-Pride. And drag shows.”

“And the guys who shut them down with threats of violence.”

“Kitchener’s not perfect, don’t get me wrong,” she says, “but I doubt anywhere is. I don’t think I could have come out in a small town. People who do are braver than I can imagine.” Celeste shivers and shoves her hands into the pockets of her jean coat. She brings her shoulders up to her ears, hiding her face behind the fluff of her collar. "Last time I was up here, I was coming out to my girlfriend. First person I ever told."

"How'd she take it?" I ask.

"Not great. Not the last person to struggle, either." Celeste shakes her head and laughs without humour. "Sorry, I didn't mean to turn our night into a trauma dump."

"I promise I'd have done it if you didn't," I assure her. "It's the only way I know how to relate to other human beings."

I drop the toboggan rope and put my freezing hands in my pockets, too. The view would be perfect if it weren't for the light pollution smothering the clear night sky. The moon shines high overhead, pockmarked and defiant.

A cloud of condensation spills from my mouth. "I'm sorry your girlfriend sucked."

"Coming out is a new gamble with every single person. People who love you say you're a whole different person. They grieve the miserable person you used to be. Even people who have no reason to care might decide you're suddenly dangerous. You know, I was nervous about you. Coming out to straight guys is the scariest."

"Hey, now. What makes you think I'm straight?"

I watch the vague surprise on her face. It's not something I go around saying to just anyone. I don't wear pins or display flags. I did technically come out on an Insta post in grade nine, but I deleted it a week later . . .

"I lost a lot of friends when I came out as bi," I say. "Now I've only got Ramy."

Her hand lands on my shoulder for the second time this week. Even through layers of winter coat and hoodie, it radiates warmth. "What am I, co-worker liver? This is an after-work social gathering, Quentin. If this isn't how the bonds of friendship are formed, I don't know how. Which could still be true. I'm friendly with everyone, but not friends with everyone, I assure you. You're lucky to have someone close."

"I guess I'm lucky in that one specific way."

"Gratitude: it's what the holiday season's all about."

I feel myself frown without meaning to. "Does the week after Christmas still count as the holiday season?"

"You bet it does! New Year's is around the corner. Good cheer hasn't been exhausted yet. Why, not a holiday fan?"

"I hate Christmas."

"*What*!?"

She looks genuinely shocked, like there aren't a million retellings of *A Christmas Carol*. Surely in one of them, Scrooge doesn't change his mind.

Once the initial shock wears off, she asks more gently, "Any particular reason?"

"Family stuff," I say.

"I feel that," Celeste says. "Christmas was hard after my dad moved out."

I wanted to hold back. To choose not to overshare. But friendships are built by give and take. I can tell Celeste talking about her dad is anywhere between a medium-to-large deal.

So I share. “It was my mom, for me. She left last year. Met somebody online. Now she’s in England.”

“Jeez. That’s tough.”

A lump blocks my throat. I don’t talk about this stuff. But at least Celeste isn’t fumbling to make me feel better. I’ve heard it all. “What did your dad do?” “I’m sure it’s hard for her, too.” “She deserves to be happy.” “It’s not your fault, Quentin.” None of it helpful.

“Where’s your dad now?” I ask. “Don’t say England.”

Celeste snorts. “He was yet another of my tragic coming-out losses. ‘Dad is stuck in his ways,’ as my mom likes to say. Sadly, those ways include a lot of homophobia and transphobia. He pretty much gave up on me after one last fishing trip failed to make me cishet. I love fishing — still a girl.”

“He sounds like an asshole.”

Celeste barks a laugh. I love her laughter. Every variation of her unplanned amusement and explosive glee. “He absolutely is. As my hat says, ‘Fish love me, dads fear me.' But Mom kicked him out quick enough. She's always got my back. I love her to death."

She fumbles in her pocket for a pack of gum, peels away the foil, and bites down. She passes me a stick of gum wrapped in foil.

"I never would have quit smoking if I didn't come out, guaranteed," she continues. "My whole life, I never thought I'd feel so okay. I thought life was misery. That everyone felt that way. And I'm not saying coming out is some magic cure for addiction. Obviously, plenty of trans people smoke. But for me, coming out made me want to live — not just survive, but actually *live.* For the first time, I can picture the future. Too many trans people don't get one."

She gazes over the cityscape as if seeing into her bright new future. I want to hug her but I don't move. We're quiet for a couple cloudy breaths.

Down in the park, someone cries, "Woo!" as their swing spins inhumanly fast.

"Wow, Operation: Give Quentin Some Holiday Joy is a bummer so far." Celeste nudges the toboggan with her boot. It slides about two feet away before I step on the rope. "How about we speed down a mountain at 120 kilometres per hour?"

Moving to the edge of the hill, I look down. My stomach lurches into my throat. One of my earliest memories is flipping the sled off of a big rock — buried under the snow, lying in wait — and breaking my wrist.

Mt. Trashmore has never stopped being scary.

Chewing the gum, icy mint turns the air sharper on my tongue, I position the toboggan a foot back from the edge. I hold it steady while Celeste sits and thanks me for "being a gentleman." Blushing way too hard, I climb in behind Celeste with my legs on either side of her while still trying to give her as much personal space as I can.

"Dude, it's too late to be shy," she says. "Snuggle up."

Wordlessly, I press my body against hers. She reaches back and takes my hands from the handles, wrapping my arms around her waist. My heartbeat could power all of the city.

I almost don't realize she's using her feet to drag us forward.

Then we're tipping.

Then we're *falling*.

Celeste screams. I squeeze her tight, the wind rushing in my ears, the snow spraying on either side of us. Vibrations crash through my body.

A jarring bump flings us into the air. The sled rotates mid-flight. My wrist throbs, the memory of snapping tendons, fractured bone. I almost swallow my gum — *why am I chewing gum*?

The toboggan slams into the ground. The gum flies out of my mouth and into the darkness.

We speed to the bottom of Mt. Trashmore like it's a bobsled race, making record time. At the bottom, we keep sliding for another half a football field, slowing until we collide with the packed, knee-high walls of snow along the edge of the trail.

Celeste and I both fall off the toboggan, rolling into the snow and laughing like we barely got away with our lives. Waiting out the adrenaline. Droplets of melted snow dot my glasses, the lights of the park smearing in a radiant rainbow glare. Once my chest calms its thunderous drumbeat, all I can hear is Celeste catching her breath. I turn my head to look at her.

She's already looking at me.

Celeste smiles, most of her lipstick faded. Her two front teeth have a small but noticeable gap. I lose myself in it, time freezing like the earth beneath us. Dark clouds drift across the moon. I almost forget how cold it is until snowflakes drift to the side of my head.

Kiss her, I think in a voice too bold to be mine.

"I should get home," I say, sitting up. My legs are cold, wet, and numb. "My cat needs insulin. Every twelve hours. He's diabetic and my dad . . . I can't rely on him."

"Oh. Yeah, for sure." I hear her getting to her feet. Not even questioning why I'd wait until midnight to give Rover his injection. "Nothing but respect for a responsible cat dad."

I can't look at her. I don't want her to know what I was thinking, to see it in my eyes. I couldn't survive the embarrassment of her rejection. I can barely survive imagining it — her hands cupping my cheeks. Her pitying expression. Her kind voice as she says, "Oh, Q, I'm so sorry if I gave you the wrong impression. Are you okay?"

I'm not some three-legged dog no one wants to adopt.

I hold the toboggan in front of me. A shield for my heart. "Do you, um, do you want me to walk you home?"

Celeste shakes her head. "I'll see you at work, Q."

She wastes no time walking away, toward Steph and her friends drunkenly swinging from the monkey bars. I lick my chapped lips and walk in the other direction.

06 Claws and Cappuccinos

"ON YOUR SIX!" Ramy shouts.

"Please don't talk like it's *Call of Duty*," I beg. "You'll ruin *Happy Town*."

Harry and Reynard swing weapons at the onslaught of holiday minions pouring from the factory. Crabcrackers — nutcrackers made to look like crabs — pinch at them, taking five Hit Points every time.

Lurking in the background, Sandy Claws perches on a throne of gifts, a crab man with fearsome claws and a beard braided with glittery barnacles. Conveyor belts pump out toy vehicles and unfinished dolls of Happy Townsfolk.

Harry's black umbrella whacks a crabcracker. Its body glows a deep red and disappears, leaving behind crab legs, Happy Bucks, and a ball of light. The light, a tiny bit of Sandy Claws's holiday magic, floats into the boss's open mouth.

Normally, Sandy Claws would never use his powers of time and space travel for evil. These are the very powers he uses to stop time on Decapodember 25 so he can deliver presents to the people of Happy Town!

I only agreed to play a combat-based quest because this is the first main story event where combat is the point. And because Ramy promised to put in a shift with me at the café afterward.

The sun shines through my bedroom window, right into my eyes. It's Tuesday morning, one of my few days off throughout the holidays, and I can't relax and enjoy it. I left my mind at the base of Mt. Trashmore.

Whenever I close my eyes, I'm lying in the snow. Celeste lying across from me. A foot of space between us, a distance so easily closed. A moment in which anything's possible.

But then I open my eyes, my stomach twisted like a wet towel. I'm in my computer chair. In the reality where that moment doesn't exist and never did. At least not the way I wanted.

"Tell me again," Ramy says, "when are you and Celeste getting married?"

"Dude," I say with all the energy of a French royal in a guillotine, begging to be spared.

"You had your first date!"

With a bonk from his frying pan, Reynard slays the final crabcracker. The whole factory rumbles. The frantic battle music stops, replaced by the intense choral music of a boss fight. Harry and Reynard look at the screen, trembling and dripping cartoon sweat, as Sandy Claws rises from his throne.

"Oh shit, here we go!" Ramy says.

Sandy Claws:

You dare dismantle my **Crustaceasmas Factory**, *snap snap*? You will pay for your insolence – in more than **Happy Bucks**!

"Does . . . does he mean blood?" I say, unimpressed.

"He means hot goss about your first date," Ramy says.

Reynard runs to the corner of the room and devours a plate of scrambled eggs, boosting his stats and healing his HP.

"It wasn't" — a claw swats Harry across the factory floor — "a date."

Ramy points at me from Florida. His long, curly hair is pinned back with a butterfly clip. "You almost kissed!"

"I said it *seemed* like I wanted to kiss her. From her perspective."

"But that's correct! You did!"

"But she can't know that!"

He puts his head in his hands and groans. "Quentin, you are literally killing me."

A swipe of a massive claw picks Reynard the Fox off the floor. Held in the air, Reynard squeaks and kicks his legs as the claw repeatedly crushes him for combo damage.

"Sandy Claws is literally killing you," I say as Harry hacks at the holiday hero's weak points, his spindly legs.

"Quentin, listen to me–"

"Can't. I'm beating this boss you begged me to fight."

"–people don't just hold your gaze under the moonlight when they don't want to kiss you."

"What I'm saying is that's my perception, though. I'm an unreliable narrator. Who knows how many seconds passed? Or how many seconds even count as holding my gaze?"

"Hopeless," Ramy says. "I can't work with this."

My *Happy Town* text notification dings. On the right side of the screen, a little red *1* appears over my DM icon. I make Harry retreat behind cover.

"Hey!" Ramy says, as Harry pulls his cell phone out of his pocket. "Are you seriously checking your texts right now?"

"Mabel messaged me," I say.

It's a couple lines from a song she's really into this week. Something we do every Tuesday.

And I never really knew
how much I'd miss you
until the grief I'd fashioned
rose from the soot and ashes,
revived anew

I smile to myself. Reynard cries out in virtual pain and Ramy in very real frustration. Reynard flings into Harry, knocking them both to the ground.

"Celeste is a verifiably real person," Ramy says.

"I've been friends with Mabel longer," I say. We met online the summer before grade ten, so we've been online friends for a while.

"We've known Celeste for *years*."

"But I've only officially been friends with Celeste for one day."

"Your definitions of, like, every kind of relationship need work."

"She agreed last night. Celeste said I'm not approachable."

"Yet she approached you anyway. Curious."

All I have left in me is an eye roll. How can you argue with someone so wrong? Ramy is just seeing patterns that aren't there because *he's* not here. Hopefully Celeste just forgets about last night.

With a final strike, Sandy Claws slumps onto the floor. He parts his beard to reveal a blinking sci-fi mind-control collar around his neck — in the shape of plastic six-pack rings — right as it snaps and falls to the floor. His eye-stalks calm. The cloudiness fades from his eyes.

Sandy Claws:

Ho, ho-HARRY? How can I ever thank you for saving **Crustaceasmas Eve**, *snap snap*?

His dialogue doesn't change even though it's days

past Crustaceasmas — I mean, Christmas Eve. But the answer to his question is loot. I earn the Sugar Plum Shield. A combat item, because they expect me to fight more of my beloved animal pals. No thanks.

"Café time?" I ask.

On screen, Ramy turns to his open guest room door and yells, "What's that, Mama? You need me to stop playing video games?"

"Are you for real?" I ask.

"And if I wanted to work in a café, I could get a real job? I'm not allowed to do fake work for no reward? Well, you heard the lady."

"I didn't, actually."

"She's the boss, man. Love you, gotta go!"

Ramy hangs up. I'm left staring at my reflection in a black screen, mouth open.

Fine. I'll work at the café by myself. And I'll enjoy it, too! Probably more than if Ramy were there! But first, I need real coffee. I fast-travel Harry back to his house, then journey deeper into my own.

My bedroom door opens onto an empty hallway,

which leads to an empty living room, in my completely empty house. Rover chirps and follows me to the kitchen.

I dump out the filter of wet coffee grounds from yesterday, and refill the machine with new grounds and water. There's still some coffee from yesterday morning in the pot, so I leave it in. The coffee machine might be as old as I am, but it dutifully hisses and grumbles as it makes its millionth pot.

This time last year, all the Christmas decorations were still up. The big plastic tree was covered with family photos in glass balls, ceramic animals, and popsicle-stick-cotton-ball craft ornaments I made throughout elementary school. Even the coffee grounds we had were festive, blends that tasted like eggnog and peppermint.

While I wait, my phone chimes. I pull it out of my housecoat pocket. The text preview says:

Mom:

Good morning, baby! Thinking of you. Hope you have . . .

My teeth clench. I put my phone back in my pocket and take a deep breath. Rover meows as if complaining that I'm not feeding him, an hour after I gave him breakfast.

The coffee machine groans like an old man who knows I'm here, but can't tell which grandchild I am. I scoop brown sugar into a mug shaped like Sonic the Hedgehog's head — the only part of him that looks at all like a hedgehog — and pour oat milk and coffee into Sonic's hollowed-out skull.

I shuffle back to my room.

One of my favourite *Happy Town* songs plays from the speakers. Cradling my warm mug, stepping into my room is like stepping into the past. A doorway to a bittersweet nostalgia.

The last couple years, I've lived so much of my life in *Happy Town*. There was nothing else to do during lockdowns and school closures. No place that felt safer. The only place where I could still see friends, even if separated by screens. Even if we only knew each other online.

I had two virtual birthday parties over *Happy Town* because people were too dangerous to be around. Because air was too dangerous to *breathe*.

Happy Town had been my escape before the pandemic, but I'd never had something so big I was trying to escape. The news was all politics and fear and death, and that was all anyone talked about.

I know playing video games can be a crutch, a way to avoid processing feelings or figuring out real life. But people need crutches sometimes, like when they break a leg. And broken legs don't always heal perfectly. Some people need crutches forever.

Sitting back down, I fast-travel Harry to the Downtown Strip. Harry materializes on a busy sidewalk with storefronts for the salon, the nightclub, the flower shop, and my favourite place, the Starbocks.

The café is full of players and NPCs, half of them sitting at tables on coffee dates, and the other half donning employee uniforms. Harry heads right for the counter, where Chuck the Rooster pours steaming coffee into a mug.

Chuck:

Good to see you, HARRY. Can I get you a **coffee**, *bock bock*?

Or are you here to pick up a **shift**?

I click the second option.

Chuck opens the waist-height door of the bar. Harry spins in a circle like he's Sailor Moon, sparkles spraying everywhere, and poses in a black polo and Starbocks apron.

NPCs line up at the counter and order their specials. A little order card appears in the top left of the screen. Harry runs to the fridge for cream, to the pumps for simple syrup, and finally to the coffee machines.

A purple axolotl sidles between NPCs Michael the Mole and Peanut the Golden Retriever.

Mabel:

can I get a flat white?

and maybe a little company?

There goes my tip streak.

Wait, what the hell is wrong with me? It's *Mabel.* I drop everything.

Harry:

sure thing!

be there in a sec

I can't actually make drinks for player characters during this mini-game, but she orders a coffee from Chuck and sits at an empty table.

I hand the last cappuccino to Tricky, the triceratops who operates the auto shop. Chuck pays me one hundred Happy Bucks and invites me back anytime.

Harry changes back to his usual sweater, orders a coffee from Chuck — because even though he is just lines of code, I need to support his local small business — and sits across from Mabel.

Mabel:

minimum wage labour but in a video game

who does that

don't you have a real job in real life?

Harry:

yeah but not at a cafe

there's something so whimsical about

like

serving coffee to regulars

remembering their orders

Mabel:

sounds like you're missing your calling

Harry:

i've applied to every cafe in my city

no starbucks will hire me

even coffee time rejected me

Mabel:

put this on your résumé

Chuck's good for a reference

Harry:

if only

it's a dream life!

i love coffee too much

i dunno

my favourite parts of happy town are the cozy parts

the boring parts

the parts that are gonna go extinct

Mabel:

extinct?

Harry:

yeah

i love this game

but things are different

happy town is one update away from PVP

if i ever join a guild, send me to the moon

Mabel:

what if I told you

the cozy bit you love
is actually the feeling of COMMUNITY
the familiarity of NEIGHBOURS and FRIENDS
which is exactly what a guild is

The axolotl sips her flat white.

Harry:
i'm assuming you're in a guild

Mabel:
you assume correctly
it's not all fart jokes and bloodlust
everyone needs their people
online or irl

Harry:
i'm still looking

Mabel:
get out there! they're waiting for you!!

Harry:

easier said than done

i'm not as cute irl as a hedgehog

i've been told i'm difficult to talk to

Mabel:

well

hedgehogs aren't exactly approachable

but I bet your lack of cuteness is debatable

I blush furiously, sipping from my own coffee. I start typing a response. I backspace. I start again. She's definitely seeing little ellipses appear and disappear.

Before I can spit out a response, she sends another message.

Mabel:

speaking of making friends and influencing people

do you want to come to a wedding?

like a happy town wedding

i've got a +1

Harry:

YES

I type it immediately, too fast. The caps lock was an unfortunate accident.

Mabel:

there will be party favours

oh, that was quick!

lol

great! it's tomorrow evening

after their real wedding

i'll send you the link to their private venue

Harry:

it's a date

i mean

not a date date

but i'll be there

I choose to stop typing.

Mabel:

lol

and then you'll have to join our guild for a raid

Harry:

wait

Mabel:

no take backs!!!

see you tomorrow ;)

07 Food, Drives

I'M NOT THE ONLY PERSON freezing my butt off outside the food bank on New Year's Eve morning. An old woman in several layers of winter coats holds the leash of a Yorkshire terrier whose bangs need a trim. A younger man with a ginger mullet and mutton chops stares straight ahead, dressed only in a tank top and shorts. And . . . there's one more person I'm not thrilled to see.

Steph Baxter shivers by the front door, hands in the

pockets of her leather jacket. "Oh. Quentin Evans. Hey."

Normally, I don't think I'd say anything. Most of my interactions with human beings consist of looking in the other direction, pretending I did not hear them, or trying to convince myself they were not, in fact, talking to me.

But I've been thinking about Celeste volunteering. And about what Mabel was saying. About community. These specific people aren't my next-door neighbours, but we live in the same city. We're here outside in the cold together, existing in this time and space. We're here for the same reason.

Even Steph Baxter.

"Hey," I say, the plastic underside of my toboggan scraping on the sidewalk in the absence of snow. "Again."

"Yeah." Steph nods at the toboggan. "Do you take that thing everywhere?"

"Gotta be prepared. Never know when I'm gonna see a mountain. Feel the call of the slopes . . . Shred. You know."

"Sure. Are you . . . here? Like, for the . . . Sorry, dumb question. I mean . . ."

"I am here for food," I confirm. "From the food bank. That's correct."

"Ah. Do you . . ." She visibly cringes, but is powerless to stop. ". . . Come here often?"

It almost makes me feel like we're on equal footing, socially speaking.

I let her off the hook. "Every two weeks for the past couple months. You?"

"First time," she says. "I don't really know how it works."

I drop the rope of my toboggan and grab a clipboard from the white folding table in front of the food bank windows. A whiteboard with a list of overflow food leans against the window. A couple cans and packaged foods are arranged in piles, each marked by a big X in Sharpie.

"Do you have an appointment?" I ask.

She shakes her head.

"That should be okay, that just means they can't

give you fresh produce. Here." I pass her the clipboard and grab myself another. "You just write your name and circle the stuff you want. The stuff on the table you can take yourself because they can't technically give you expired food."

Steph makes a face.

"But it's fine to eat," I say. "Oh, and you can pick two things from the whiteboard. They'll usually ask if you want more than two."

Tucking her hair behind an ear red from the cold, Steph says, "Thanks."

"For sure. Happy to help. The first time's the scariest."

She smiles uncertainly. "They usually are."

The door swings open, and a middle-aged East Asian woman hands a reusable grocery bag to the old woman with the dog. "Here you are, that's the last one. And here are your milk vouchers." She hands slips of paper to the man with mutton chops before smiling at me, her face framed by her black bob. "Good morning, Quentin."

"Morning," I mumble.

I always feel guilty when people know my name and I don't know theirs. My brain is famously bad at holding such vital information. But only one of us writes our name for the other every two weeks.

Food Bank Lady turns to Steph. "I'm sorry, I don't think we've met."

"First time," Steph says. "I'm Stephanie Baxter. Quentin gave me the rundown."

"That's very helpful, Quentin. Thank you," she says. "Maybe you can earn some volunteer hours here. We're always in need of more people power."

"Maybe," I say, handing her the clipboard and my empty grocery bags.

"I'll be right with you, Stephanie," she says, and goes inside.

Waiting in silence with someone you only kind of know is a uniquely painful part of life. Would it be more awkward to continue saying nothing, or to risk trusting my mouth to say something worth sharing? What would a normal person do?

Snow crunches under tires, and a teal minivan crawls into the parking space we're standing in. Steph and I both back up in opposite directions.

I can't believe who's in the driver's seat.

The van door opens and Celeste says, "Whoa. I didn't expect to see either of you today, let alone both. Lucky me, eh?"

This trip to the food bank is a cosmic prank.

Steph looks as uncomfortable as I feel. Going to the food bank is hard enough without seeing anyone you know. There's a culture of shame built around being poor, but it's worse when you're poor and willing to accept help. We're supposed to shut up and pull ourselves up by our bootstraps (a thing that is impossible, literally the point of the saying originally).

Celeste opens the trunk of her minivan and carries a crate of groceries to the door.

"Do you want help?" I ask.

"Totally, Q," she says. "Grab what you can carry."

I go to the open trunk, lined with green crates

full of cans, produce, and toilet paper. Steph steps beside me and picks up a crate of boxed pasta. Out of a misplaced sense of masculinity, I grab the handles of the crate of cans and drag it closer, heaving it off the edge. I try not to groan as I waddle inside.

"Thank you, darling." Food Bank Lady cups Celeste's cheeks and kisses her forehead. "You're an angel."

Even for Celeste, this level of friendliness is otherworldly.

"You're welcome, Mom," Celeste says.

. . . I guess that makes more sense. Food Bank Lady is Ms. Eguchi. (Though I still don't know her first name.)

A young guy emerges from the back room. I know him from somewhere, too. "Hey, all of these bean medleys are out of date."

His biceps bulge as he holds a crate of bean cans with way more ease than I ever could. He faces me with a dazzling grin and it hits me. He's the guy from Celeste's background on her phone.

"Need help?" he asks me.

"No," I grunt, short of breath. "Just . . . tell me . . . where . . . "

He gestures to a table. I slam the crate down. Arms noodling, Celeste hands me two full grocery bags. I rush back outside before I can embarrass myself any further, and drop the bags in my toboggan.

Of course Celeste's hot boyfriend would be here, too. I can never come to the food bank again. It's a cursed place.

I go back to waiting silently, shifting my weight from foot to foot. Steph tucks her clipboard under her arm and takes out her phone, which is a great idea, but I don't want to look like I'm copying her.

From Steph's phone, music plays. I know the song immediately.

"You play *Happy Town*?" I blurt out.

She looks at me, blinking. It takes her a moment to say, "Everyone and their grandma plays *Happy Town*." Then, less harshly, "I mean, yeah. Like, every day."

"Me, too," I say.

What are the chances someone I know from school plays *Happy Town*? Have I ever played with her without even knowing it? I'm positive a normal person would be able to turn this into a half-hour conversation. I could spout *Happy Town* trivia for days. But we say nothing else.

After a couple minutes, Celeste brings me my third bag of food. "I had no idea you knew my mom! And behind my back, too."

I shrug. "I didn't know she was your mom. I guess it makes sense, with the meal centre thing."

"It's the same organization."

"So you work here, too? I haven't seen you around."

"Mostly I drop off the donations from people in the neighbourhood, and from food drives. I'm collecting from some local grocery stores today."

"You're, like, an actual angel."

She smiles wide, not disproving the theory. "Are you testing out pick-up lines, Q?"

"I mean, like, a saint." Very different vibes. Saints

are all old men sworn to celibacy, right? "Next you'll tell me you go carolling."

"There is nothing charitable about carolling," Celeste says seriously. "No one wants to stand on their cold porch, nonconsensually listening to you sing out of tune."

Ms. Eguchi opens the door and hands me my last two bags. "There you are, sweetie."

I thank her and add them to my toboggan pile. One of the bags slumps over, spilling loose potatoes into the grey, tire-smushed slush. Crouching, I pluck them out of the muck and shift the bags so they lean against one another with more stability.

"Did you walk?" Celeste asks.

"Yeah," I say.

"But it's, like, an hour away."

"Two, if you consider having to go back home."

"Why didn't you take the bus?" she says with a disbelieving chuckle.

"Why didn't I get on crowded public transport with fifty pounds of grocery bags? So everyone can laugh at me while my apples roll up and down the aisles?" It makes my neck itchy just to think about. "No thanks."

"All right, get in the car. I'm taking you home."

"I couldn't–"

Celeste holds a finger up to silence me. "I'm going to insist, but only because I know you're an anxious, self-sacrificing martyr who says no to things you'd really like to say yes to because you're afraid of imposing on anyone else."

I'd be stunned into silence, if silence weren't my natural state.

After a satisfied moment, she says. "That's what I thought. Put your things in the back. Steph, don't tell me you walked."

Steph looks up from her phone. She takes her hand out of her pocket and jingles her car keys.

"All right. Mom!" Celeste calls, snapping me back to reality. "I'm driving Quentin home!"

"Drive safe," Celeste's mom says, taking the clipboard from Steph.

Celeste starts the engine while I load my things into the back of the minivan. I climb into the passenger seat. Celeste smiles and waves at Steph. The hot guy salutes from the back of the room. After a quick social calculation, I keep my hands in my lap and don't look at anyone.

Celeste reverses and we're on the road. She turns the volume dial, but it's not ska this time. She's listening to that famous *Star Wars* song, the theme of the bad guys. For fun.

"If the other cars could hear you, they'd be terrified," I say.

Celeste grins. "You think so? Doesn't everyone casually listen to 'The Imperial March'?"

We stop at a red light. A car stops beside us on my side. Celeste's left hand goes to the window controls and the windows slide down, cold air rushing inside the car. With her right hand, she cranks the volume.

"The Imperial March" blasts so loud my ears might bleed. It takes all of my courage to look at the driver next to us.

But they're not mad. They're laughing. Then they're head-banging, long hair whipping back and forth, fingers held in devil horns like it's a metal song.

The light turns green. Celeste quiets the music, raises the windows, and drives.

"How do you even make friends in traffic?" I ask. "The road is for angrily honking and saying other drivers are bad at driving even though you all have the same basic qualifications."

"Do you normally trigger road rage in other drivers?" Celeste asks.

"I don't drive."

"Why not?"

"Never learned." I shrug, hands in my lap. "I was supposed to, but my parents never had the time. Then Mom left the country. Dad's always working, since keeping our house isn't easy with half the income, and Mom being between jobs means no child support. Hence you find me at the food bank."

"That really sucks, Q. I'm sorry."

"It does." No sense pretending. I appreciate that

she doesn't, either. "You really listen to this while driving?"

"Absolutely. John Williams will play at my funeral."

"I guess you really like *Star Wars*."

"Oh, you've noticed, have you?" she asks, one hand under her right ear. She wears lightsaber earrings, one red and one green. "*Star Wars* is the best. Hell, *space* is the coolest. That's why I picked the name Celeste, because it comes from the word *celestial*."

"I like that."

"Thanks," Celeste says. She's quiet for a moment before she brings the conversation back to *Star Wars*. "Have you watched *Andor*?"

I shake my head. "I've only seen the one with Jar Jar Binks."

"Oh my God, that's criminal. You're under arrest. You need to watch *Andor* immediately."

"I don't have a lot of streaming services."

"Then you'll have to come to my house. I'll rewatch it a tenth time just for you. Not tonight, though. Sadly, I am busy."

"Me, too," I say.

She smiles like she doesn't quite believe me, but it's one of the few times it wouldn't be a lie. I do have a wedding to go to. In my computer. Between two people I do not know.

Celeste pulls into the empty parking lot of the Halt N Purcha$e. It's only a five-minute walk through the trail to my house. Unbuckling, I say, "Thanks–"

"Don't thank me yet," she says with a smile I can't decipher. "Welcome to your first driving lesson."

"What?" Heat rises up my neck as I watch her walk around the car and open my door. "No. Why? What?"

"First tip: sit in the driver's seat."

"I can't drive."

"That's the point. Come on. What's the worst that could happen?"

"I crash your car. The nice lady at the food bank's car. You fly through the windshield and die. George fires me for damaging the store. Your mom bans me from the food bank. I starve to death. When I get to

Heaven, you kick me out of the sky for revenge, and I spend eternity in Hell."

"Impressive catastrophizing. Now, what's the best that could happen?"

"I dunno."

"I'm not going anywhere until you drive me around the parking lot."

I grumble but ultimately find myself behind the steering wheel, fastening the seat belt.

Celeste tells me to adjust the side mirrors until I can see just the top of a sliver of the back doors, and the rearview mirror until I can see the whole rear windshield. I move the seat back. I turn the key in the ignition until the engine rumbles to life.

I feel like a mech driver suiting up for the first time, except I'm definitely going to anticlimactically crash into a kaiju and explode. Roll end credits.

"How much do you know about driving?" Celeste asks.

"Nothing," I squeak. "Tell me everything there is to know."

"Once you put the car into drive or reverse, the car will move if you don't have your foot on the brake pedal. Not fast, but still."

"Didn't know that. Learning already."

She leans close, one arm across the back of the driver's seat, a hand over one of mine on the steering wheel. Every thought about driving flees my head. My whole body goes full supernova.

"This okay?" she asks, inches from my ear, her breath crisp as a winter morning.

I can only nod.

With Celeste's instruction, I press my foot down on the brake and shift into drive. The car jerks forward, then rolls slowly out of the parking spot. "Great, take it nice and easy. Next, to accelerate, press on the gas. Lightly–"

At the tiniest tap of my toes, the car lurches forward. We speed toward the Halt N Purcha$e storefront.

"LIGHTLY. LIGHTLY. BRAKE. BRAKE–"

My foot jumps to the brake and kicks down hard.

The car stops instantly, but our bodies don't. I jerk forward worse than any sudden stop of a city bus, the seat belt cutting into my chest. Adrenaline rushes through my whole body. I'm breathing hard, close to hyperventilating.

Through the Halt N Purcha$e window, our manager stares at us in horror.

Laughing, Celeste waves at George. "You passed your first lesson."

I turn to her, sure I heard wrong. "I did?"

"First lesson is how not to crash a car. You did it. A+."

08 Happily Ever After

CHAI AND CHAMOMILE are getting married in the middle of the One Thousand-Acre Forest, home of Happy Town's loveable local politician, Mayor Grizz. The mayor himself wanders aimlessly around the clearing in the middle of the forest, where the crowd of wedding-goers form small groups, or take a seat in the rows of white, floral chairs (from the wedding event between NPCs Lizzy the Rainbow Chameleon and Valerie the Vampire Bat.)

In the real world, it's 10 p.m. on New Year's Eve. I've finally stopped feeling like vomiting from the memory of my driving experience — her hand over mine, her face so close, my death rushing toward me. Ramy, despite being every bit the *Happy Town* addict I am, isn't online tonight. He's probably with his family on a beach somewhere, watching real fireworks. Poor guy.

Harry sits on a chair near the back, in a black suit I bought him just for the occasion. Everyone seems to know each other already. No other players talk to me. It's a little too much like the awkwardness of real-life parties.

Mabel is nowhere to be seen.

What if she stood me up? Maybe she got an invite to a real party for New Year's. Or maybe she invited me to the wedding of people she doesn't even know as a cruel joke.

A red door in a tree trunk swings open, and a purple axolotl steps out of it. Mabel wears an orange dress with puffy shoulders. She runs over to the brides first, emoting with cheers and confetti party poppers.

Then she heads right for Harry. I make him stand,

like a proper gentleman. Mabel messages me in our private chat.

Mabel:

you made it!

Harry:

wouldn't miss it for the world

I'd pressed Send before it sunk in exactly how desperate I sound. I try again.

Harry:

because you needed a +1 so bad

And now I'm negging her. Shit shit shit–

Mabel:

lol thank you

i really do appreciate it

can I get you a drink?

Harry:

i'd love one

As she goes to the bar, I wipe my sweaty palms on my jeans. The last thing I need is for my computer mouse to suffer water damage because my constant state of nervousness makes me the sweatiest human on Earth. Mabel returns with two flutes of sparkling Celebration Juice. I equip it into Harry's paw, and he taps his glass against Mabel's.

Harry:

how do you know the brides?

Mabel:

we actually met here when i was in grade 6

they were so flirty, everyone saw this coming

even me, and I was only 11 lmao

they got married earlier today but keep saying this is their real wedding

a fairytale internet love story

My whole body lights on fire. My brain goes fuzzy from a flood of fantasies. I'm short-circuiting too much to find anything meaningful to say.

Settling for something less meaningful, my woefully sweaty fingers tap my keyboard.

Harry:

that's wild

Mabel:

it totally is!

short-distance relationships are hard enough

Harry:

i bet

Mabel:

what, not a player, mr. hedgehog?

Harry:

never been in a relationship

i'm not dating material

Mabel:

whoa now

what does that mean

Harry:

i dunno

i used to get bullied

girls asked me out as a prank

because the idea of dating me was funny, i guess

Mabel:

oh hell no

screw those girls, they SUCK

you didn't deserve that

and everyone deserves love!

Harry:

easy to say

Mabel:

it's true

everyone

even those assholes who bullied you deserve love

maybe they'd be nicer if they got any

I chuckle to myself.

Harry:

maybe

A horse in a priest's robe stands before the crowd. In the public chat, he says:

Arnold:

Attention everyone, the ceremony is about to begin. Please take your seats in an orderly fashion.

Harry follows Mabel and the rest of the guests. Arnold steps toward a pipe organ set up in front of Mrs. Acorn's carpentry workshop. After a moment, the organ plays "Here Comes the Bride," and Arnold moves to the wedding arch. Chai, a pink turtle, and Chamomile, a white rabbit with red eyes, take their places on either side of him. They wear identical white wedding gowns.

Arnold:

Thank you for joining us to celebrate this happiest of unions.

We gather today in the forest that started it all, where The Coconut Ducks formed and our guild leaders felt that first spark of *something more*.

I'm sure I speak for everyone when I say it has been an honour to watch your romance flower, blossoming a little more with every bug caught, MacGuffin found, and boss defeated.

Chai and Chamomile have written their own vows to share.

Chai:

My beloved, never in a million years did I imagine I would fall in love when I downloaded *Happy Town*. Fall in love with adorable NPCs, maybe, but not start a relationship – a relationship that has lasted years, survived IRL hardship, and been an enduring source of joy. Happy Town has been our home, but even more so, you've been my home. Thank you for sticking around even though the first thing I said to you was, "You are dead wrong." I can't wait to embark on new journeys together. I love you.

The crowd of wedding guests politely type lol.

Chamomile:

When we met in this forest, I was the loneliest ninth grader in the world. I wasn't looking for love – mostly because I thought I would have to marry a boy, and boys were gross, which meant love was gross. But then I joined your guild, The Coconut Ducks, and met you. We immediately argued about which dragon is the best. You convinced me to start watching *Dragon Ball*, and I got you to begrudgingly watch the 1996 classic *Dragonheart*. You won the argument. And I knew I was wrong about so much more: I'm a lesbian and love is awesome, actually.

Another round of lol appears above the crowd, joined by a single LMAO!! The avatars of the players all do the clap emote. An elephant in the crowd rises from their chair.

Babar:

I LOVE LOVE

The couple walks down the aisle, paw holding claw. Arnold stands before the pipe organ, and the music and vibes change dramatically. A bouncy pop song crackles through my speakers. It's a real song, re-recorded in the gibberish language all the *Happy Town* NPCs speak. All the animal guests pick a dance popular enough for the devs to have added to the game, flossing and Griddying and everything else this side of TikTok.

Everyone but me and Mabel.

Mabel:

what are you thinking about

Harry:

i'm just

worrying

Mabel:

a favourite pastime of yours ;P

Harry:

ha yeah, surprise

i worry sometimes about getting too attached to people

like online people

it's all just the internet

Mabel:

no such thing!

Harry:

i worry it's not real

Mabel:

either everything is real or nothing is

sure, you've gotta go outside sometimes
but the friendships you make online aren't less real because they're online
it's about the time and care you put into it
hours spent talking and bonding
that's valuable
that makes life worth living
i value our friendship, Harry
i know i don't know your name
or your face
but i know what you show me, and I know the time we've spent together, and I trust you
that's the only way to live
finding people you trust

Mabel runs to the dance floor. After a quick reconfiguring of my emote shortcuts — I never use the dancing emotes — Harry joins her.

Before I know it, it's almost midnight. New Year's Eve.

Ding. Mabel sends me another message.

Mabel:
Happy New Year

The axolotl holds her arms open. I click the hug emote and Harry leans in, wrapping his arms around her. Alone in my room, I feel like the whole world can see me blushing.

An automated message takes over all the NPCs. Mayor Grizz leads them in a collective shout.

Mayor Grizz:
Happy New Year!

The camera pans to the night sky. Fireworks shoot among the stars, exploding into blossoming colour. Outside, I hear something similar — the fizzle and whine, pop and crackle of neighbours setting off fireworks in the park. Explosions of merriment, unless you're a dog, or a veteran, or the environment.

Another point for virtual celebrations, I think.

Maybe I need to forget all the weird shame I've

built up around online interactions — it hasn't stopped me from spending most of my time on the internet. Sure, there are lots of awful places on the internet full of awful human beings. But not here.

Not tonight.

09 More Like Mayor Grillz (Me About Life)

I'M LEANING AGAINST the window of my train car, watching our departure as we crawl out of the station, when there's a knock to my right.

Mayor Grizz:

Oh, hello there. Is this seat taken? It's always a joy to meet a new friend on the train, don't you think?

The bear stands in the doorway of the train cabin,

adjusting his waistcoat. It's Mayor Grizz. The Mayor Grizz from *Happy Town*. His dialogue box even says so. This is normal and fine.

I'm not sure I agree with him, but I'm not picking a fight with a bear. I don't remember how I got on this train to begin with.

???:

I guess so.

Oh. I haven't chosen my name yet.

Mayor Grizz shuffles sideways through the doorway, taking a seat across from me.

Mayor Grizz:

Thank you kindly, young man. I'm Grizz, mayor of Happy Town! It's a lovely place. Not as quiet as it used to be, but even the coziest of homes must change eventually. What's your name?

A transparent keyboard appears in between us.

Hesitantly, I tap the keys hovering in the air, spelling *Q-U-E-N-T-I-N*. I poke Accept.

Are you sure? asks a text bubble prompt. You cannot change this later.

Should I have said Harry? I don't know. I tap Confirm and the keyboard vanishes.

Mayor Grizz:

Pleasure to meet you, Quentin. Where are you from?

Quentin:

Kitchener, Ontario.

Mayor Grizz:

And why did you leave?

Quentin:

What?

Mayor Grizz:

You're running away, are you not? Why else would you be

on a train with no luggage, no plan, and 500 Happy Bucks in your pocket?

I pat my jeans. From my right hip pocket, I pull out a wad of green Happy Bucks.

The train car rumbles and sways. The countryside flies past, all chunkily rendered fruit trees and small farms made of pixels. A groundhog's shovel bites into the soil. They take off their wide-brimmed hat, wave at us, and are left behind as we charge forward.

Quentin:

I guess I just like Happy Town better.

Mayor Grizz:

But Happy Town isn't real.

Weird thing for the mayor of Happy Town to say — what's he mayor of, then? But a piece of advice surfaces in my mind. Words without a voice. I don't remember where I heard them — or read them?

Maybe an inspirational poster somewhere.

Quentin:

Either everything's real or nothing is.

Mayor Grizz:

But, Quentin, have you put in enough effort to make anything real?

In the cabin across from us, Chuck the barista sips a cup of coffee, and Ms. Waksberg, my math teacher from fifth grade, reads the newspaper. They both wave at me. This also seems normal and fine. I wave back.

Then I see them. At the end of the train car, both facing away from me. On the right side of the aisle, green hair. On the left, the purple frills of an axolotl.

The train rumbles harder. There's a squeal of metal, a lurch of the car to the left, and the countryside out the window shrinks away, sectioned by squares of different shades of green and brown like a quilt made of dirt. The train is *flying*. Fear grips my chest. I can't breathe.

Mayor Grizz:

Something the matter?

Quentin:

I'm afraid of heights.

Mayor Grizz:

Are you? Or are you just afraid of falling?

Quentin:

What's the difference!

Mayor Grizz:

Finding out what happens at the bottom . . .

Mayor Grizz shrugs. The train angles upward, barrelling into the sky. Pressed into my chair, I find something to hold on to, squeezing the cushion of my seat as if it can save me. The train seems to slow, the window showing more space than Earth, and then . . .

My heart leaps into my throat.

We angle downward.

I scream.

Quentin:

We're gonna die!

Mayor Grizz:

That's the way the honeycomb crumbles.

The mayor's sombre voice echoes as darkness seeps into our cabin, swallowing Grizz, and me, and everything.

***

I open my eyes to more darkness, my heart pounding. Something heavy covers my mouth and nose. I can't breathe.

Swatting at my face, my hand strikes the softness of my pillow, and behind that, the twenty-five pounds of pure fluff that is Rover. I sit up, drenched with sweat. My alarm clock screeches.

"Meow," the attempted murderer complains, before hopping to the floor and waddling down the hall.

"Jesus," I say.

Rubbing my face way too hard, I try bringing myself back to life — for the last time, if Rover has anything to say about it. It might be time to lock Rover out when I go to bed . . . but I could never. He's my emotional support animal. My best buddy. I've drawn too much *Happy Town* fan art of him.

Tossing the curtains open, I'm greeted by the view of my backyard. The hammock sags under the weight of the freshly fallen snow. Little paw prints wind through the buried garden and around the tall maple tree. It's the first day of the new year, and my first real emotion is anger at Mayor Grizz.

I grab my glasses, open my messenger app, and video call Ramy.

He doesn't answer the first two times. On the

third, his face is half-hidden by his pillow, his eyes shut. "Blah," he groans.

"I feel like I'm cheating," I say.

"On who?"

"Not even, like, on a person. On *Happy Town*. Or on reality."

He scrunches up his face. It takes him a second before he says, "That's insane."

"I know! That's why I'm telling you!"

"But I'm sleepy."

"And I'm having an existential crisis!" I say. "Mayor Grizz is guilting me in my sleep!"

". . . What?"

"Meanwhile, you're partying in the party capital of the United States."

"Hey, I'm fighting for my life down here. A gator keeps stealing my clothes from the clothesline! It got my commemorative *Animal Forest* tee!"

"Florida is not a real place."

"Take it up with Florida Man. Worry about your own reality."

"Again, that is why I'm calling you! The sooner you help me deal with it, the sooner you can go back to sleep."

Ramy groans and flops onto his back, holding the phone above him. "Fine. But you do feel like you're cheating on a person. That's the core issue. You just can't admit that you can't figure out what you want."

"I know what I want," I say. "I want somebody to love me for who I am. Like, romantically. And then clearly state that they do — again, romantically — because I don't want to guess and be wrong. Is that too much to ask for?"

"Have you considered that other people want the same thing?"

"Impossible."

"And anyway, you need to love yourself first, my man. How can you expect anyone else to put up with you if you can't?"

"Harsh."

"You can only hear the frequency of my voice when it's harsh. Quentin, listen to me." Ramy sits up, his curly hair falling in his face. Uh-oh. He might be taking this more seriously than I was actually prepared for. "You are a kind, smart, attractive guy. Okay? Too many people have tried to convince you otherwise. The girls who bullied you in Ms. Waksberg's class were mean. They do not determine your worth. And Max and Julian and Thom don't know shit about being good friends or good dudes. They chose to miss out on your brilliance."

Unable to meet the intensity of Ramy's support, I turn to the window. To the hammock sinking under the weight of snow and memory. My chest swells from the pressure of a secret kept too long. A secret I've kept even from Ramy.

Max's face, inches from mine. Leaves rustling overhead. Our fingers brush–

"I never told you," I say. "Max was right."

"What do you mean?"

"It wasn't a rumour. I did try to kiss Max. We were lying on the hammock. I told him I was in love with him. I kissed him. He even kissed me back. But then he got all weird, and he walked home, and didn't talk to me all summer."

I look back to Ramy, expecting . . . well, I dunno, anger? Disappointment? Validation that I am the bad guy, and always have been. But that's not what I see on Ramy's face.

"And then," Ramy finishes for me, "you came out online. And Max commented the worst comments human garbage could come up with, Quentin. He didn't do that because he was a good guy."

"But I kissed him. I ruined our friendship."

"A good guy would have said, 'Oh, Quentin, I don't feel that way, but I'm your friend and I'm here for you.' It's as simple as that. He chose the path of villainy. He chose to forever miss out on your richness of *soul*, brother."

I sniffle, a big lump calcifying in my throat. "You only call me brother when you're trying to make me cry."

"Crying is good for you. You have value, Quentin. I can think of two people who agree with me. Celeste is into you. Mabel is also into you. You need to either ask one of your unofficial girlfriends out, start reading about polyamory, or move on to someone who wants to date you. Stop making excuses and start making decisions. You might like how it feels."

"As opposed to how this conversation–"

"Love you, goodbye now." Ramy blows me a kiss and hangs up.

There's a sharp knock on my door. It's loud and, because it doesn't happen much anymore, I jump. "Hello?"

Dad takes that to mean "come in" and opens my door. "Let's have breakfast," he says.

He's wearing clothes, so he must be about to go to work. Normally I barely get a goodbye. The air smells like bacon.

My stomach rumbles. In spite of it, I say, "I'm not really hungry."

"Eat what you can, then," he says. "Sit with me."

"At the dining table? It's covered in paper."

"Is that so?"

He walks away. With a sigh, I stand up.

The table is not, in fact, covered in overdue bills and unopened mail. Instead, there are two plates with eggs, bacon, toast, and two mugs of black coffee. Dad sits at one spot and pushes the oat milk and sugar closer to my spot.

"What's the occasion?" I say, sitting down.

"Do I need a special occasion to eat breakfast with my son?"

I purse my lips and poke my egg. Yolk runs yellow and thick over the crispy white. I hate runny yolk. "I was joking. Because it's New Year's."

As if he doesn't believe me, he looks at the calendar on the kitchen wall. "Oh. So it is."

Dad slurps his coffee. Our forks scrape our plates. The kitchen clock ticks unusually loudly. I do, in the end, take small bites of my toast, at least the bits that didn't get any egg on them, and the bacon. The silence is torture.

When I finish my bacon, I stand up. "Well, thanks."

"You've hardly touched your–"

"What is this?" I interrupt. "Why are you doing this?"

He sits back, frowning. "What do you mean?"

"I mean you can't check out for twelve whole months and then decide you're my dad again. You haven't been here! I've been doing our dishes and our laundry and picking up food all by myself, all year, without hearing a 'thank you' from your spot on the couch!"

Setting his coffee on the table, Dad avoids meeting my glare. His thick eyebrows furrow, like he's genuinely confused. "I . . . I've been working, Quentin. To keep a roof over your head."

Carefully, my voice trembling, I say, "I appreciate that you're working hard. But don't pretend it's all for me — not when I never asked you to. Not when I'm working, too. Not when I still need a dad sometimes, man."

He says nothing, staring straight ahead into his breakfast. I run my hands through my hair and stop before I tear it all out. I take a deep breath before I scream. I don't want to hurt him, but I'm so angry, so tired of feeling lonely in my own house.

"Mom is gone and she's not coming back," I say, cutting right to the core of all our problems. He flinches like I hit him. "I think . . . I think she's happy. We can't ignore reality just because we wish things were different."

I don't wait for a response. I march to my room and lock the door behind me.

Sitting in bed and doing nothing, I listen as his chair scrapes the floor. The keys jingle. The front door shuts. The engine of our car grumbles to life, and fades into the distance.

10 Community IRL

GEORGE STILL HASN'T NOTICED the missile toad.

Working on New Year's Day isn't my first choice, but at least I'm making more money because it's a stat holiday. And the practical reality is that I do not have a life, no matter how much I would rather be at home playing video games.

Unfortunately, no one else wanted to work. This means George joins me behind the counter — or rather, he's been kicking me out from behind the counter so

I can sweep, mop, check the expiration dates on the milk, check the temperature on the freezers, and so on, even if all these things were done an hour ago. I can't even touch my phone pocket without George demanding I straighten a shelf.

The more meaningless tasks I'm given, the more I'm stuck inside my own head. Replaying this morning over and over, trying out different words, exploring different outcomes. Heart pounding the whole time. I hate conflict. When I get angry with someone, I struggle to turn it off until either there's a definitive end to the fight, or we both silently agree to never talk about it again.

Knowing how my dad's been lately, it'll probably be the second option.

I love my dad. Of course I do. My chest aches with guilt for being so harsh. He's been going through his own shit, obviously. But everything I said is still true. It's still how I feel. I just . . . I miss *before*.

"Quentin," George says. He snaps his fingers, pointing at the shelf of cookies. He says nothing more, so I just go down the aisle and pick up Oreos like I'm doing something.

George knows how to harsh a vibe. It must be instinct. Ancestral memory, coming from a long line of managerial sapiens. Growing legs, crawling out of the primordial waters, and saying, "If you can lean, you can clean" at the beginning of time.

I've been mentally preparing myself not to rat out Celeste all day. Steeling my will like a criminal in an interrogation room. *I'll never tell you who took the mistletoe!* But no, every half hour he postures behind the counter, surveys the room like an overlord, and says nothing about the flying amphibian.

Despite his dictatorial tendencies, the worst part of working with George might be the music. We've listened to the radio for *hours*. The classic rock station. Hours of middle-aged men making dad jokes, Boomer observations, taking phone calls from people who think they're prepared to talk on the radio but are really, really not, and then playing "Life Is a Highway." George hums or sings under his breath the whole time.

I miss Celeste's playlist. I've even branched out from Celeste's suggestions and found some ska on my own. I have an informed opinion now, and I've come to one conclusion: as annoying as it might be to ska fans everywhere, the mozzarella sticks meme is correct.

The problem is, the meme assumes the connection between ska and mozzarella sticks is that they are childish, and that childishness is bad. The same criticism is said about *Happy Town*. But I think what's considered childish is actually pure *joy*! Even bursting with content that's considered bad for you — like anarchist punk themes or just so much cheese and oil, respectively — both are so undeniably joyous.

Mozzarella sticks taste like the best parts of childhood. Ska sounds like a carefree summer. Neither should be written off as a joke.

Outside, all the snow has melted. As much as I am not a fan of winter, I also am not a fan of climate anxiety. I have enough anxiety, thank you. I'd much rather have to suffer through normal, miserable winter than worry about how the planet has been dying for decades and no one is stopping it because money matters more to them than people in Africa taking the worst of climate change to the chin.

Mt. Trashmore must be a big mound of mud. Hardly the beautiful place it is in the snow. Or in the summer. The kind of place where you can lie in the grass beneath the stars and stare at your co-worker's pretty face.

Celeste smiles, showing off the gap between her two front teeth, and all I want is for her mouth to be closer–

"Can't get no . . ." George mumbles. "Satis-*faction . . .* "

"Can I go to the washroom?" I ask.

He scrunches up his mustache. "Make it quick," he says. "I need you to reorganize the beef jerky. I'll be having a stern talk with whoever put Teriyaki to the left of Original."

I go to the back and lock myself in the washroom. Finally, a moment to myself. Sitting on the lid of the toilet, I take out my phone.

Maybe it's being trapped here with George. Maybe it's the stress dreams about wasting my life. Maybe I just really want to see Celeste.

I google the address of The Souper Centre.

***

After my shift, I hop on the next bus heading toward downtown. In five minutes, the bus stops in front of a church tucked away in the suburbs across from Mt. Trashmore, and I hop off.

I know the area. In grade seven, Ramy dated a girl who lived nearby. She had a basketball hoop in her driveway. I was always the third wheel and never, ever allowed to leave without him because Ramy didn't like basketball . . . or girls.

Opening the church doors, I'm blasted by the warmth of the foyer. My stomach growls, because I haven't eaten since breakfast with Dad. I follow the scraping of cutlery against bowls, the laughter of people enjoying conversation over hot food, to the main room. The air is heavy with oil and humidity, fragrant with spices. Long folding tables with chafing dishes line the area in front of the stage, and smaller dining tables teem with people.

Celeste leans against the back of a chair, chatting with a couple of regulars I know from the Halt N Purcha$e. She laughs and gestures animatedly, entirely in her element.

At another table sit a couple of unhoused downtown regulars who always ask passersby for a pop or chocolate bar from the stores that have banned them. I even see a couple of people I know from school, some serving food and others seated together, eating soup — and, because the world is an unfair place, Steph Baxter is here too, with her new GSA friends. I reflexively pull up my jeans.

As if Celeste and Steph both being present didn't make me anxious enough, the hot guy from Celeste's phone background uses his biceps and charming good looks (and a ladle) to fill the bowls and bellies of the underprivileged. A real Superman type.

Why did I think coming here was a good idea?

I turn around and step back into the foyer when Celeste says, "Quentin!"

Warm fingers wrap around my freezing hand. I stop, looking down at our hands together, our skin touching, just to make sure it's real. *Celeste is holding my hand.* What does it mean? Does it mean anything? Friends hold hands sometimes, right?

Because I've been staring at our hands for way too long, I look up. She's wearing a black t-shirt with white text that says *BURGER & MEISTER & MEISTER & BURGER*. She's also looking at our hands, for some reason, before she meets my eyes and lets go.

She puts her hands on the hips of her black skinny jeans and smiles. "I'm so happy to see you!"

"You are?" I ask before I can stop myself.

She laughs and says with a certainty strong enough to convince even me, "Yes, I am. You didn't tell me you were coming."

"It was impulsive, I guess."

"Wow, I didn't know you could act on impulse.

I must be changing you like a proper Manic Pixie Dream Girl."

She grins, so clearly, she's said something clever. Unfortunately, I say, "I don't know what that is."

"Don't worry about it. Are you here to eat? Or would you like to volunteer?"

The place does smell delicious, but I say, "I'd love to help if you need any."

"Always. Johnny needs a break anyway."

A pit settles in my stomach as I follow Celeste behind the counter, right to the obscenely hot guy I now know as Johnny.

"Your prayers are answered. I've brought backup," Celeste says. "Johnny, this is Quentin."

"Whoa, *The* Quentin?" Johnny asks.

"Shut up," Celeste says.

"I've heard so much about you, The Quentin."

"You have?" I ask, because I really can't stop myself from speaking before thinking. I can't tell if I'm being made fun of.

"Celeste talks about you all the time," he says.

"She does?" I've never felt more like I've just wandered out of a 1920s psych ward post-lobotomy.

"Okay, you need to go." Celeste gets behind Johnny and pushes him away from the counter. "Goodbye now."

"Pleased to *finally* meet you, Quentin." Johnny grins and, even though he's in a hairnet and clear plastic gloves, I can't help but fall in love a little anyway. How am I supposed to compete with Celeste's secret boyfriend when even I am not immune to his charm? "Grab a hairnet. See you in fifteen."

Fitting her own hairnet over her green hair, Celeste says, "Take your time."

I just nod, finally able to shut myself up, and do as Johnny says. I grab a hairnet from a box and put it on. I wash my hands and dry them with paper towels. People form a line, holding empty bowls. Waiting for me.

Picking up the ladle, I'm struck with fear. The only thing worse than not volunteering would be to mess up volunteer work so badly they ban me for life.

But what am I going to do, run away?

The person next in line clears his throat impatiently. Steam rises from the chafing dish. Peas, lentils, shreds of chicken, and cubes of carrot float in the ruddy broth.

Looking over my shoulder, Celeste nudges me with her elbow. "Go on," she whispers. "You've got this."

I take a deep breath, apologize, and empty the ladle into his bowl. He thanks me. Moves along the line for Celeste to plop a dinner roll onto his tray. She smiles at me, and the next person takes his place, and we do it all again.

Some new people come in from the frozen night to where the soup is warm and the vibes warmer. Most people ask for the chicken noodle, but there's Thai peanut soup for the herbivores. I fill bowls for adults and children, for the people of my community, each connected to me the same way as everyone at the food bank. We're here together. People helping people.

Mabel might be right. It might be the sense of

community that I love most about *Happy Town*. That I'm missing most in real life, especially with my home so empty. There's a warmth in my belly, a comfort in my muscles, a gratification I haven't felt in a while — despite the pangs of hunger.

Once there's no line and Celeste and I are alone, I make the mistake of opening my mouth again. "So," I say. "How long have you known Johnny?"

My probing is not subtle. It is also not voluntary. Just word vomit I can't help but hurl.

Celeste snorts. Then, like a joke that becomes funnier after chewing on it, a second laughing burbles out. "Pretty much since birth."

"That's a long time," I say.

"I'm sure you wouldn't understand, but that is generally how siblings work."

I . . . am not very smart.

Hoping to hide the surprise on my face, I look down and stir the soup. "I have heard rumours. What's that like? Having siblings?"

"It's like being assigned a roommate at birth. Your

first friend and your first enemy. Johnny's annoying as hell, and I love him to death. Pretty much all of my favourite things were his favourite first, until I stole them."

"I still haven't beaten *Kingdom Hearts II*," Johnny says behind us.

"Oh, because I loved spending time with my big brother?" Celeste asks.

"Exactly. You ruined it by loving it too much."

"You never were any good at sharing unless Mom made you."

"Why should I have to?" He takes the ladle from her. "You already stole all of her attention."

They both stick their tongues out at each other, as deadly serious as Old West cowboys in a duel. I think maybe Johnny wins because he's pulled down one of his bottom eyelids, something I've only seen anime characters do.

"Joke's on you. Now you've gotta wash your hands." Celeste straightens and grabs two empty bowls. "You good to take over?"

"Yup. Have fun, you two."

"Shut *up*," she hisses.

She fills both bowls with chicken noodle soup and passes me one. The soup heats my hands through the porcelain.

I don't really like chicken noodle soup. Or any soup. I mean, I eat it anyway, because when you can't afford groceries, you get what you get and you don't get upset. But it's not my first choice.

Celeste leads me into the greater cafeteria. The tables are all pretty full. All except for Steph's.

"Hey, guys," Celeste says. "Mind if we sit?"

Steph looks at her, then at me. She smiles tightly. "More the merrier," she says without enthusiasm.

Sitting between Celeste and the guy from the park with the pink buzz cut, the group at the table at least acts like that's true. They resume their conversation about the new *Final Fantasy*, which no one could afford and which everyone, including me, desperately wants to play. It's probably the easiest conversation I've ever joined.

I bring the spoon to my mouth. The broth scalds my lips. Flavour blooms on my tongue. Warmth spreads through my belly. It's nothing like the chemical-yellow concoction I think of when I hear "chicken noodle."

"Oh my god," I say. "This is the best soup I've ever had."

Celeste leans against me, bumping into my shoulder. "Thanks!"

"You made this? Like, from scratch?"

The rest of the table says, "Whoa," or "Holy shit," or "Celeste, this is *so good.*"

Celeste smiles wide, sitting up straight and proud. "Made my own stock and everything. I love making soup. You take the garbage you would throw out, and turn it into so much food, to feed so many people! And it brings up all these feelings of comfort. Memories of parents and skipping school and watching game shows, all the things that make being sick sufferable. There's nothing better than making soup. Except for people complimenting your soup, of course."

"Celeste, hun?" her mom calls from a couple tables over. "Come here a second?"

"Bee-are-bee," Celeste says, scooching back from the table.

With Celeste gone, I'm drowning without a boat in a sea of human interaction. I focus on eating my soup, listening to a dozen different conversations around me, until Steph says, "Quentin. Can we talk?"

My gut unclenches. I didn't realize I'd been waiting for this. For her to say I need to find a new food bank, *or else*. For the middle school bullying to continue. I should leave before she pantses me or something more severe, more high school.

But I just nod. She stands and motions for me to come with her into the foyer, and then to the parking lot. I should have grabbed my coat.

"I'll be quick," she says as if reading my mind — or my rigid, shivering body language. "I've been thinking a lot. About the past. About who I've been, and who I am. And I think . . . I know I wasn't kind to you when we were kids. For a long time, I just thought it would be best if I never brought it up. We could go the rest of our lives never talking. You could remember me that way forever, and even if it bothered me, it didn't really matter, you know?"

Steph toys with her braid, facing the parking lot. I'm tempted to agree with her and end the conversation. But I also think about her bullying too much. It feels pathetic to admit, but what she did when we were kids still bothers me. I'm holding on to ten-year-old anger.

"But now we keep running into each other," she says. "And I know what it's like for people to be shitty to you for stupid reasons. Since my mom got laid off, my oldest, closest friends have noticed I'm acting differently, dressing differently, bringing different food. It sucks. They suck. And I'm sorry that I sucked, Quentin. I was a bully. I'm not proud of it."

Unclenching my jaw, I nod. It's a better apology than I ever expected. Better than I knew I wanted. I don't know what to say.

"Can I hug you?" Steph asks.

"Oh," I say. "Uh. Yeah. Sure."

I open my arms. She moves in. But we both clearly favour the same side, and we almost bump our heads together. Then we both apologize, step back, and adjust the other way. Her hand smacks my ribs. My hand lands awkwardly on her waist. My mouth is dry. I pray for a meteor to strike us down.

She steps back and holds me at arm's length. "You should just . . . just stand still."

"Good idea."

Holding my arms wide, I wait for her to fit into my embrace however she likes. Her cheek rests against my chest. Her arms around my waist. We hug for a breath, two, three. The church doors open, light falling over us. Steph and I break apart.

Celeste stands in the doorway, her smile tight. "Sorry, didn't mean to interrupt."

Steph pats my shoulder. "No worries. I hope we're good?"

Celeste looks at me for confirmation. I give two thumbs up, as if possessed by a socially awkward demon.

Steph sidesteps past Celeste, through the doorway. I hold the door so Celeste can go first, and I join them at the table once more.

And it feels different. I'm lighter. I talk easier, though it's still far from easy, and I still second-guess everything I say the instant it leaves my mouth. But no one tells me to leave. Steph and I add each other on Insta. I'm eighty percent sure Pink Buzzcut even laughs at one of my jokes.

Maybe the meteor can hold off for a bit longer.

11 On Manic Pixie Dream Girls

AFTER A QUICK GOOGLE SEARCH and a couple of hours spent watching movies that came out between 2005 and 2015, I think I understand what a Manic Pixie Dream Girl is.

She usually has coloured hair and piercings, though I think that used to be edgier and less common. She has some Big Theories About Life, which she teaches the shy, depressed, pretentious main guy in order to convince him to *really live, man*. She's a quirky splash of colour in a world made black and white by boredom. She's less of a person and more of an idea — one time literally, in that movie where the guy is a writer and she is made up.

Celeste was joking, probably. She obviously looks the part. But I think when you're a lonely, sad, scared guy, every girl who gives you attention is in danger of becoming your Manic Pixie Dream Girl. Maybe that's all my crush is, in the end. Me imprinting on Celeste because she's nice to me in real life.

She deserves better than that.

With the movies running on my phone, I'm also doing chores and quests in *Happy Town* on my computer. Harry waters a patch of strawberries in his extensive fields, fenced in and guarded by differently dressed scarecrows. A Direct Message *ping*s for my attention.

Mabel:

you ready?

Harry:

i guess so!

An invite to a raid pops up. I click Accept and my humble farm disappears. The game loads onto Badger's Gate. Mabel's guild, The Coconut Ducks, gathers outside a massive ornate arch with giant wooden doors and the carvings of two snarling badgers on either side.

Chai:

oh hi Harry!

we meet again

Harry:

lol hey

thanks for the invite

can't wait to bonk a badger

Yes, I finally caved and gave a guild another chance. Yes, when Ramy finds out he will razz me to death because I'm doing it for Mabel . . . which is why

I blocked him. Temporarily! I'm not actually joining a guild. I'm like a supporting character. A volunteer.

Outside my bedroom, the front door shuts. Dad's home early. He hasn't really tried another bonding attempt. It's probably for the best.

Once everyone confirms in the guild group chat, Chamomile goes up to the gate. It swings open and we file into the arena. Boss battle music plays. The stone floor in the centre of the arena cracks open and a giant badger claws her way to the surface. Like with Sandy Claws, an electronic six-pack ring wraps around her neck, red light blinking.

A long red HP bar stretches across the top of the screen, over which reads the boss's name: *Boisterous Badger.*

The guild scatters. Marksman-class players shoot stones and explosives from slingshots. Magic users feed healing stews to friends and throw freezing ice cream cones at foes. I guide Harry alongside Mabel and the other melee combatants, charging close and hacking at the badger's paws. Every time Harry swings his umbrella, numbers appear above it to show the damage he's dealing.

Chamomile:

dang harry, coming in clutch with the vorpal sword

snicker snack

Chai:

cham

Chamomile:

sorry i have a problem

an alice in wonderland problem

Chai:

we're all mad here

(our apartment)

A rush of warmth rises to my cheeks. Sure, raiding still isn't my favourite. But this guild and their positivity is the exact opposite from Ramy's. Volunteering every so often might be fun.

After about twenty minutes, the remaining inch of HP bar blinks, the final attacks are dealt, and the mind-control litter snaps away. Sparks shoot from the device's exposed wiring.

Boisterous Badger:

Thank you, HARRY. The Forest is in your debt. I will let the other Spirits of Nature know what manner of technology is being wielded against us by the vile Mega Corp.

We're rewarded with a high-defence Badger Cap, and the titan burrows into her underground tunnel system. Guild members thank me for my help, send me friend requests, and disappear from the arena.

Then it's just Harry and Mabel.

Mabel:

want to come to finish up my New Year's quests?

Harry:

for sure

where to?

I tail her to several spots on the world map. She trades a diamond thimble for Travis Toad's lost wallet under the awning of the Solace Salon. She gives Travis his wallet and he's so grateful he offers her two free tickets to the Malamute Merry-Go-Round — which we could use, but Mabel knows it's a better deal to trade these tickets to the will-they-won't-they NPCs Cherry and Apricot, two dogs who live on opposite sides of the suburbs and always talk about their secret crushes on one another.

Mabel:

well, I'm done

and with half an hour to spare

want to chill at The Octopus's Garden?

Harry:

race you there

As soon as I hit Send, I click on the Octopus's Garden icon. Harry loads in a good five seconds before Mabel appears. I'm making him floss in victory, gloating.

Mabel:

that's a dirty trick, Harry

I click on the beach, and Harry runs to a blue beach towel, sitting down and facing the water. Mabel sits beside him on the same towel. On the distant island stage, the octopus slays a drum solo and the crowd cheers. The Flamingo Ferry trudges along back to the dock.

Mabel:

hey, so . . .

i wanted to talk

My body immediately launches into panic mode. Lizard brain activates. Should I be afraid or excited? Is there even a difference? I type back with shaking fingers.

Harry:

you can tell me anything

Mabel:

lol intense

Harry:

sorry

Mabel:

not in a bad way

but it's a personal thing

i know we try to avoid personal things

i know that was my idea

and . . . this is kind of why

Harry:

i said anything

i meant anything

My heart hammers in my ears and fingertips and every part of me. My mind balloons with every possibility. Mabel confessing she's been catfishing me. Mabel confessing her plans to take over the world, and I get to be her sidekick. Mabel confessing her undying love for me.

Ellipses cycle, left to right. It takes a thousand years for her message to reach me.

Mabel:

i'm trans

It's almost a letdown, because it's no big deal. Or it shouldn't be. But I recover my wits enough to know this isn't about me or what I think, not really. If she's sharing this now — the way she's sharing it now — it's a big deal to her.

Harry:

cool

wait no that sounds sarcastic

i mean that's awesome

i mean

thanks for telling me

for trusting me

Mabel:

i'm sorry i didn't tell you earlier

i wasn't trying to hide it from you or

or trick you

or anything like that

i just liked being able to be me, without any qualifiers

and i didn't know you yet

like, i was an axolotl and an internet stranger

my personal identity wasn't anyone's business

that felt like enough

at first, anyway

but we kept being friends

and then we became pretty good friends!

it felt like it was too late to tell you

in case you stopped liking me

Harry:

i could never stop liking you

It might be the most honest declaration of my feelings I've ever shared. With Mabel, but also with *anyone*.

Mabel:

you're not mad?

i was so afraid you'd be mad

Harry:

why would I be mad?

Mabel:

it's just, like, a thing

the trans person tricking people into liking them

i didn't want to trick anyone

but when we met i was only just starting voice training

i hadn't even transitioned socially yet

Harry:

Mabel, seriously

first of all, you were right

it's nobody's business unless you want to make it their business

i'm your friend

and i'm not going anywhere

and that's that

Little sparkles appear over Mabel's head.

Mabel:

you're the best

Harry:

that's what all my reviews say

We sit like that for a while, not typing, barely

panicking, until the half hour runs out and she has to go to bed. Alone, Harry watches the digital waves, and I just . . . think. No, that's not right. I think all the time, to the point of overthinking everything. This is different.

I decide.

After this conversation, this shared intimacy, I have some clarity. I know what I want. I want to take a chance on this girl.

Harry leaves the beach and rushes to the general store. He buys frog-themed stationary (because there isn't any axolotl print) and opens it there in the store, with other players milling about.

Once I start typing, I can't stop. Everything pours out. I tell her my real name. I attach my phone number. I say I know this might be crazy, but I need to take this chance because I've been scared for too long — because I've secretly loved her for two years. But no worries if you don't feel the same! (I'm still an anxious wreck, and it's not like I can't take no for an answer.)

Palms sweaty, out of breath, I guide Harry to the post office next door. Pick Mabel on my Friend

List. Pay the five Happy Bucks to send it. The pigeon behind the front desk assures me the letter is on its way.

I log off and shut down my computer. I throw my phone out of reach too, so I can't obsessively check for a response. Even though I told her to call me. Like everything about my brain, it's a paradox I can't think too much about.

Like, for instance, the fact of my breathing getting shallower.

She doesn't like me.

I chose this. I made a choice for once! But I'm getting less air with every inhale. My lungs are a bucket I'm trying to fill, but someone's poked holes all over and the water is leaking everywhere. It's not fair. I wanted this, I know I did, but my stupid brain is punishing me.

She'll never love me.

I breathe in but it does nothing. I can't get a lungful. I might pass out. I could die. And no one would find me for days.

Why the hell did I send that letter?

I wrap myself in my blanket. Tears of frustration and fear trickle down my skin. I struggle to breathe for what feels like forever, waiting for the panic attack to pass.

12 A Missile Toad to the Heart

"IT'S SNOWING AGAIN!" Celeste kicks the snow off her boots on the brick outside, before stepping wetly onto the soaked front mat. "It's a Christmas miracle."

"It's January third," I say. "When do Christmas miracles expire?"

"Never. That's the magic of Christmas. It's always Christmas in here." She taps her temple. "Last weekend of the holidays, though. Ready for school?"

"God, no. But I've never been ready for school a

single day in my life."

She folds her long coat and sets it on the plexiglass protecting the lotto tickets. "Ah, a fellow Dishonour Roll student. Is it anti-establishment? Or maybe anti-intellectualism. Quick, is the Earth flat or round?"

"It's more like anti freaking out all the time. I have never, not once, volunteered an answer in class. But teachers see me and think I'm some underchallenged gifted kid just waiting for my chance — that, or they just think it's unfair for the others that I don't raise my hand. So they call on me. And I never have an answer. I never have any idea what they're even asking. My brain gets all fuzzy, and I can't think of anything but literally running away. It's just humiliating for everyone involved."

"Hm." She crosses her arms, leaning with her butt against the counter. "You've mentioned anxiety being something you deal with a lot."

"Basically, every day I constantly feel like I've done something wrong and I'm seconds away from being publicly humiliated."

"Have you tried anti-anxiety meds?"

I shake my head. "My parents aren't, like, against medication, but they both think getting a diagnosis is 'a little hasty.' But I never pushed too hard. And the idea of medication makes me nervous. I don't want negative side effects."

"That's a valid concern," she says with a shrug. "But what about positive side effects?"

Honestly, I'd given those much less thought. Due to the anxiety, probably. I just shrug.

"I'm on a couple different meds," she says. "Estrogen, Prozac, trazodone. And yeah, I know lots of people who quit their meds because of side effects. Sometimes they try new meds. Sometimes they try going without. Everyone's different. I got lucky. On meds, I feel more like myself — or at least, more able to control who I want myself to be, you know? I think it's easier to choose which path is best when you can actually see the map."

"You make a compelling argument," I say.

"Obviously, looking into therapy is also a good

idea. And another hard sell."

"My dad wouldn't have time to take me to therapy."

"Does he need to? I thought you were doing basically everything yourself. You can consent to your own care."

"That's true. If only I had the money."

"You could try CMHA. They have free counselling," Celeste says. "Anyway, I'm not trying to impose. Mental health is hard to talk about, and harder to do anything about. I see you getting all tense."

Am I? I drop my shoulders and pry my teeth apart. It's so automatic, tense is my default state. Nothing about the fog of anxiety even feels unusual, no matter what's causing it. "Sorry, I–"

"No need to apologize."

Celeste takes out her phone. No matter how our relationship has changed in the past week, I still have the superhuman ability to make things too weird to keep a conversation alive. And I can't distract myself with my own phone. Just feeling my phone in my pocket makes me a little panicky and sick. Like looking at my phone would make my brain literally melt out my ears from the pure, weapons-grade embarrassment of rejection.

Stupid hormones. Stupid love letters. Stupid . . . me.

I've already deleted the *Happy Town* app. Then redownloaded it. Then deleted it again. And then — well, you get it, on repeat several hundred times.

There's no way Mabel hasn't read my letter. She knows how I feel. No wiggle room, no ambiguous author intention. And she hasn't responded.

I can never log onto *Happy Town* again. Or use the internet. I'll spend the rest of my days sleeping under this counter, scratching lotto tickets until I'm a millionaire and I can move far, far away.

"Q?" Celeste glances up from her phone. Her cheeks seem a little redder than usual. But she says nothing.

"Celeste?" I say.

She must not be feeling well, because she shakes her head and asks, "Do you mind mopping today?"

Nodding, I get up and head for the supply room. Celeste doesn't usually ask me to do stuff she's supposed to do unless she's having nicotine withdrawal issues, or if she's sick.

I splash cleaning solution into the yellow mop bucket and fill it with hot water, soap bubbling into thick, foamy suds. Wheeling the bucket between the aisles, I slap the wet mop on the floor.

Busywork is the worst for getting out of your own head. As usual, I'm stuck overthinking. Turning over my letter to Mabel like a Rubik's cube, twisting phrases in the confession. Finding an alternate future in which she at least responds to me.

I finish up and dump the bucket of grey, grimy water down the sink in the back. Then, because Celeste is still on her phone and quiet, I grab the window cleaner and microfibre cloth.

Chemicals spray across the frosty glass. The glass clears beneath my hand, ice shavings gathering on the cloth, the muscles in my shoulder already starting to burn. Standing under the mocking missile toad, which seems to say, "Better luck never. Ribbit."

I scrub the glass harder. In the reflection, I see Celeste standing behind me.

Under her breath, she says, "Screw it."

I turn around, mouth open to ask what's up, and she cups my face in her warm hands. I look back and forth between her eyes, each a rich brown, unwavering as she studies me. Stepping into the personal bubble that separates strangers from friends from lovers, Celeste leans in. Her lips press against mine. Soft, and warm, and minty.

And then I realize, *she's kissing me.*

It's not butterflies in my stomach — the wing beats are too strong, the fluttering too numerous. Her lips are the spark that light a fuse for my insides, causing a chain reaction of popping and fizzling and sparkling like New Year's fireworks. The kiss ends, her breath hot on my lips, her eyes searching mine once more. They must find what they're looking for, because her lips fall on mine again.

My own lips move on instinct, as if they've been

studying, waiting for this moment. Matching her movements and giving in to the instinctual nature of kissing. But the rest of my body second-guesses everything, my brain overheating with worry. Am I standing too far back? Do I shuffle closer? Can I put my hands on her hips, or run my fingers through her hair? My hands ask for stage directions while her own excavate like well-travelled explorers, utterly comfortable on my body despite being total strangers.

The scene operates on dream logic. In what real world would Celeste — cool, sexy, vaguely hardcore co-worker Celeste — kiss me during our shift? Under full view of the cameras and the storefront windows? *What is happening?*

Mostly, I'm in shock. I have to be. That's the only explanation for why, eventually, I pull away.

"What–? Why did–?" I can barely get out a whole sentence. Every urge in my body begs me to undo the damage, to reattach our faces, to flood my brain with endorphins, but I can't. "Where did that come from?"

She studies me for a long, silent moment. Her eyebrows furrow gently — not quite offended, but hurt. I've hurt her.

She shrugs and looks away. "I thought you . . ."

She stops. Not the soliloquy I was hoping for. The silence curdles like a carton of milk forgotten under a shelf.

"Listen, Celeste," I say before I can stop myself, a great idiot train barreling into the station. "I think you're cute, and funny, and cool, and selfless, and awesome. I like you. Like, *a lot*. But I . . . I'm in love with somebody else."

She barks a laugh. As if she can't possibly imagine that there might be other girls I'd have a shot with. My face gets hot enough to explode.

"Are you serious right now?" she says.

"Y–yeah, I am. I know it's dumb, but I wrote this letter, right? And I–"

"This was a mistake. I'm sorry, Q."

She squeezes past me and storms outside. Clocked out early. The wind slams the door closed, the breeze spinning the missile toad in dizzy circles, dooming him to fly off course.

Celeste keeps walking, leaving me all alone, fingers on my tingling lips.

13 Sledgehammers of Knowledge

THE TROUBLE WITH CHOICES is they're always followed by consequences. But it's too late to take my choices back, and I'm done hiding from consequences. I log onto *Happy Town* as soon as I'm home.

Harry wakes up in bed. He rushes downstairs. Throws opens the front door. Opens the mailbox.

The empty mailbox.

Worst-case scenarios are always the easiest to imagine. Maybe Mabel's been murdered by her secret husband and buried in her rhubarb patch. Or she's on the run from a shady government agency because only she has the nuclear codes, as discovered through elaborate *Happy Town* puzzles. Or Mabel signed up to go to Mars at the last minute to escape the climate crisis.

Or Mabel just . . . doesn't like me back. And I turned down someone cool in real life who I really like, for someone who might not exist and is totally ghosting me. Only I could have messed up this bad.

I take a moment to smother myself with a pillow, a moment in which Rover decides it is appropriate to sit on top of that pillow and actually smother me. I flail for my life, then get back to the game.

I write Mabel a DM. A DM that keeps getting longer and more rambly. I delete it a couple times. Simple is best.

Harry:

heyyyy

I wait. After five minutes, it still doesn't register as read, but the little green dot over her picture means she's online. Maybe the message is too simple?

After ten minutes, I look for her.

The marketplace is full of lions selling ornate rugs, crows displaying fine art, a mosquito trading a bag of coffee beans to a panda. Downtown, a digital protest marches past City Hall. The nightclub is packed, but she's not there, either. Harry runs in and out of the café, the museum, the sky palace, all with nothing to show for it.

Because there's only one place I should be looking for Mabel. The place that carries the weight of our friendship entirely on its shoulders. The place I'm most afraid of going right now. It's time.

I hold my breath, scroll through the locations menu, and click The Octopus's Garden.

Mabel sits on a bench overlooking the ocean, her legs swinging. A single tentacle lashes at the sky, then returns to the water with a splash. The digital sunset fills the sky with colour.

Harry:

found you

Harry stands at the edge of the garden, seaweed topped with rose and tulip and violet petals dancing in the artificial wind, but she says nothing. She could be AFK. Heart hammering in my ears, I make Harry sit beside her on the bench.

Harry:

i'm sorry for making things weird

we can pretend it never happened

i don't wanna be just another creepy dude on the internet, y'know

it's just, ur important to em

me* lol

please say something

Mabel:

it's not your fault, quentin

i wasn't who you were expecting

Harry:

what do you mean

i don't have any expectations

i just want you

Mabel:

then why didn't you

nevermind

i just

i thought kissing you would go differently

that's on me

I stop. My eyebrows meet in my confusion. Time in this timeless place grinds to a halt just long enough for it to hit me. The knowledge is a sledgehammer to everything I thought I knew.

Mabel's not some girl I need to board a train to find. The two girls I've been obsessing over were one girl the whole time. How didn't I notice? Why didn't she tell me?

Harry:

oh my god

celeste

i am an idiot

Mabel:

no you're not

Harry:

i'm coming over

Mabel:

wait wut

NO YOU'RE NOT

Harry:

doing it

don't even know where you live

wandering out into the snow

getting my hypothermia on

i'll be waiting @ halt

Mabel:

don't you dare

But I've spent too much of my life not daring.

I grab my coat from the front hall closet, shove my arms into its sleeves. Dad's snoring on the couch, asleep in the middle of *The Muppet Christmas Carol*. I take the half-full beer can from his limp hand before it becomes a mess. I pick a fuzzy throw blanket off the floor and lay it across his body.

He's got bags under his eyes big enough to hold a video game character's inventory. His beard is bushier than it's been my whole life. He opens one eye a crack.

"Quentin," he says.

"Sorry," I say. "I was just tucking you in."

"You were right," he mumbles. "You deserve better. Better than this. Better than what I . . ."

He stops talking. His breathing deepens. A snore gurgles in his sinuses.

I head out.

It's a five-minute walk to the Halt N Purcha$e,

but the wind and snow and cold make it feel ten times longer. I wrap my scarf tighter around my neck, tuck my chin behind it and my jacket collar, ball my fists in my pockets.

She might not come. I can't blame her, not when I can barely see down the sidewalk and my toes have already lost all feeling. My sneakers sink through unplowed snow, my legs freezing from the knees down. A sniffle shoots icy mucous up my sinuses, stinging like pool water. It really had to be the coldest, snowiest night of the year.

The ever-glowing outdoor light above the Halt N Purcha$e beckons me like a lighthouse and finally, I reach the cover of the plaza's alcove. I check my phone. The clock turns over from 11:59 to midnight.

And there she is, bundled up beneath the street lights.

14 The Proper Pronunciation of Axolotl

SHE CUPS HER HANDS in front of her mouth, exhaling a cloud of smoke. Before I know what I'm doing, I'm running toward her, shouting, "No!"

She turns around, dropping her hands. Hands that are empty. "What?"

I stop running, skidding in the parking lot slush. "I thought–I thought maybe you were smoking again. And it was my fault."

"Dude, I'm just warming up my hands. You

thought I was smoking again because you rejected me?"

"I didn't reject you — I mean I didn't mean to — it was just because — but . . . yes."

"Quentin, if I start smoking again, it is no one's fault but my own."

My chest contains the bass line to every metal song ever recorded. My heart might just explode and ruin everything. She closes the distance between us, her toque frosted over with snowflakes, and I can't stop imagining her lips on mine. Holding my breath until she kisses me again.

Only, she doesn't kiss me. She shoves me. "You–"

"I know," I say, my hands up in surrender, "I can't believe me, either. I can't believe I rejected the prettiest, coolest girl I know because . . . because I was already in love with her."

"If you just like how I am online . . . If you don't like me for me, because I don't look or sound or–or, I dunno, smell how you expected, because I'm not someone like Steph–"

"Steph?"

"You know. White, cis, gorgeous. You've been getting close . . ."

I swallow, remembering when Celeste walked in on Steph and me hugging. I never would have guessed that would make her insecure. "The other day, Steph was apologizing for bullying me when we were kids. She was, like, the main girl who picked on me."

"No way! Do I need to talk to her?"

I grab Celeste's hand. Her fingers are warmer than mine, at least. "It's settled. And I think *you're* gorgeous. I've had a confusing crush on you all year. But we only just became friends. I've been in love with Mabel for longer, and I couldn't just say, 'Sorry, I take back my love letter because my co-worker kissed me.' I didn't know."

She snorts. "All right. I guess having principles is a pretty good excuse, Harry the Hedgehog."

Now, she kisses me.

The warmth of her melts away the snow, and the cold, and the threat of limb loss due to frostbite. She smells like mint, and fresh-baked cookies, and under that a little sweat from hurrying however many blocks to get here. My hands fit on the curve of her back. I pull her close. Her hands cup my face and her fingers enter my tangle of soaked brown hair. This kiss is like returning to a home I didn't know I had. It's every timeless sunset moment in The Octopus's Garden. I never want to part.

But she's the one who pulls away this time. Hand still on my cheek, she grins and mutters, "So, in love, huh?"

"I mean, uh . . ." I stop myself from apologizing for how I feel. From running from the consequences. "Yes. Shamelessly. I'm in love with an axolotl."

"It's actually pronounced ah-show-loat," she whispers, like it's romantic. "Rhymes with *goat*. It's a Nahuatl word — that's what Aztecs spoke." At my expression, she says, "What? Amphibians are one of my special interests. Don't get me started on amphibians in *Star Wars*. Grogu almost committed genocide against Frog Lady's people, man. It's not too late to run away."

"Never."

"Good. But there is only one way to shut me up." She leans in close to my ear, whispering, "Did you know axolotls can regrow their gills, limbs, and even parts of their brain–?"

Per her recommendation, I make her shut up. With my mouth.

We kiss for what feels like the most glorious forever, until I can't feel the tip of my nose, ears, or anything else. Eventually, even though I could keep kissing her for-literal-ever, we both decide we should probably take a breather. We lean against the door of the Halt N Purcha$e, her head on my shoulder, watching the blizzard cover the parking lot.

"It's a weird relationship origin story," she says. "In love before we ever met. A couple of video game animals."

"My parents were high school sweethearts and they couldn't make it work. I don't think there is a right way to fall in love." I kiss her forehead, feeling braver, more daring, than I've been. "Besides, I think it was right for us."

"I wouldn't change a thing." She nudges my shoulder with hers. "Now that you know my secret identity, is it weird if I ask if you want to hang out tomorrow?"

"In person? At your house? In real life?"

"Yeah."

"I was just gonna hang out with you online anyway. It's a date."

The snow lets up, and I pull her away from the door and walk her home. She doesn't live far at all. We share one final pulse-pounding kiss good night.

I don't remember the last time I was so excited for tomorrow.

15 Gifts

I SIT UP WAY TOO STRAIGHT on the couch in Celeste's living room. A serving platter of freshly baked cookies lies across the coffee table. Every inch of space is occupied by Christmas decorations.

It's weird seeing Ms. Eguchi and Johnny both casually wandering around, but it's far from the worst awkwardness I've ever endured. They're both kind to me, and inviting, and Ms. Eguchi keeps offering me more food that I accept politely. (After saying no the first three times she asked, because even being invited over by my girlfriend — that's right, I have a *girlfriend*, something I found out after awkwardly confirming we're exclusive — I can't stop feeling like I'm imposing.)

Celeste is wearing a t-shirt of Frog and Toad, from the children's book series. The amphibian love runs deep. When I commented on it, she said proudly, "They're gay. I love them."

"Really?" I ask. "Like, fanfic gay, or canon?"

"Like, written by a closeted gay man gay. Frog and Toad have big 'and they were roommates' energy."

"Don't get her started," Johnny says from the other room, holding a Switch in front of his face. "You have no idea long she can talk about gay shipping."

"He's just mad about my Heat Miser and Snow Miser headcanon," Celeste says.

"They're brothers!" Johnny says.

"*Step*-brothers in the first movie."

"Still bad!"

"In the olden times, queer folk deceived the public by pretending to be 'good friends,' roommates, and yes, even relatives–"

"Please stop."

"They fight like ex-husbands. I just think it's all an act, or a problem with censorship of children's media like in the *Sailor Moon* English dub–"

"Quentin, I'm begging you, do something."

Celeste was right when she said I wouldn't understand siblings. Laughing, I stay neutral as they bicker and tease each other.

Hands in candy cane–themed oven mitts, Ms. Eguchi tells us dinner is ready. We have turkey and mashed potatoes and other holiday leftovers. A Christmas redo.

At the table, Celeste sits beside me and passes me a shiny present. "Merry Christmas."

"It's not Christmas," I say.

"It's always Christmas in my heart, Quentin. Get with the program."

"But I didn't get you anything."

"People don't give presents to get presents back. And besides, yes, you did." I look at her, confused, and she rolls her eyes. "It's your love, Q."

"Oh. Right. You're welcome."

"Well? Open it!"

I look up at the others around the table. "I don't want to be rude . . ."

"Nonsense," Ms. Eguchi says.

I pry open the gift wrap as carefully as I can, and open the lid of a cardboard box. Inside is a pair of stuffed animals. A hedgehog and an axolotl.

"I've been crocheting these for a couple months," she explains. "I didn't think I'd ever be able to give them to Harry the Hedgehog himself."

"I love them. They're perfect. But I think I want you to keep Harry." I pass her the hedgehog. "I'll keep Mable. That way, we'll always have each other around."

Celeste's tawny cheeks turn as rosy as I've ever seen them. "That is the sweetest thing I've ever heard."

"Very smooth," Johnny says, nodding sagely.

Setting the box under my chair, I lean against Celeste. "I've been wondering," I whisper, "when did you know? That I was Harry?"

"Other than when you told me, an internet

stranger, all of the personal details of your life?"

Blushing, I poke the mound of potatoes. "Yeah, other than that."

"I've been collecting evidence. Keeping an eye on you since I found out you play *Happy Town* at all. But . . . I'm not any better a detective than you are. I had a crush on two equally lovely boys for a long while." Her fingers lace between mine. "If you like feeling emotionally stable, I do not recommend it."

***

When I get home, Dad's on the couch as usual, but there's something different about him. He's wearing pants, for one, even though he doesn't work today. For another, his face is clean-shaven, and he's got little balls of toilet paper marking where he nicked himself with the razor. Most shocking of all, he's drinking a glass of *water.*

There's an uncanny-valley effect to the scene. Dad, but not. Something sinister pretending to be my father.

"Hey, bud," he says as I kick off my shoes.

I hang up my coat. "Um. Hey."

"Can we talk for a sec?"

"Am I in trouble?"

He laughs. "I'm the one in trouble. Can you sit?"

I sit on the other end of the couch, cross my legs, and face my dad. I glance at him, unable to tell what that expression is, before I look at the carpet and pick a stain to focus on.

"You were right the other day," Dad says. "I've been checked out. I justify it with work. Work means money. Work also means I'm exhausted, so I always have an excuse to be alone. Being alone means neglecting my son. I've been . . . It feels dramatic to say, but I've been grieving. The death of my marriage. It's not your fault. Never has been." Dad leans forward, clasping his hands between his knees. A white ring of indented skin stands out on his ring finger, where yesterday he'd still worn his wedding band. "I'm sorry, Quentin. I want to try harder."

I nod, a lump forming in my throat.

"I think . . . I think we've both been mad at your mom for too long," Dad says. "It's not her fault, either.

Not all of it. Everyone just wants to be happy, and sometimes we can't be happy with the lives we have. You can stay miserable forever, or you can change your life. I'm going to make some changes. She messaged me, by the way. You haven't been responding to her."

"Yeah."

"No one can make you forgive her. But it's not her fault I've been acting like an asshole. I just want to make that clear."

"Okay."

"Can I have a hug, Quentin?"

He stands up and I stand up, too. We hug. It's weird. It's nostalgic. It's been a long time.

"Wanna do dinner tonight?" he asks. "I was thinking pizza."

"I like pizza," I say.

"Great. See you then."

He pats me on the back and I resume my regularly scheduled march to my room. I sit in my office chair, booting up my computer. My phone buzzes in my pocket.

Mom:

Hey, babycakes. Miss you. Would love to have a video call sometime. Or a normal phone call. Or an email. Do you have my email? I love you.

I take a deep breath.

It's not all her fault. I know. I guess I've always known.

I type a message.

Me:

I love you too, Mom.

She replies instantly with a Bitmoji version of herself shouting, "Yay!"

Happy Town loads up. Harry stretches his little arms and goes downstairs. Mabel's already seated at his dining room table. My messenger app rings and I answer.

The video chat shows Celeste's grinning face, a smile hot enough to melt my heart in my chest. "Hey, stranger."

ACKNOWLEDGEMENTS

Here we are at the end of my second Real Love book, and I have my own IRL and virtual communities to thank.

I'm very grateful to the team at Lorimer for their continued support. My thanks go to Allister Thompson, Morgan Wright, Susan Adlam, Kristen Hahn, Bradley Myles, Daniel Campbell, Joe Stacey, and James Lorimer. Extra thanks to cover designer Tyler Cleroux for his work on the most important part of the book.

Eternal thanks to my wife, Miranda Moth, for reading *Lonely in Happy Town* first, saying too many nice things about it, and telling me to change the café name to Starbocks.

Thank you to Lisa Para for saying my last book was "worth reading on the toilet" when I needed inspiration to write a book in half a month. And again for saying this book was even better than *Losing Hit Points*.

Thanks to Write Club — Miranda, Lisa, Vanessa

Ricci-Thode, Bones McKay, and Ursula Gray — for being a click away when I need to complain about how writing is hard.

Thanks to Jer Hunter, and their YouTube channel Skatune Network, for making me realize ska is awesome, actually. And to Reade Wolcott, lead singer of We Are the Union, for writing "Boys Will Be Girls," which is the song I describe in 03. Listen to the album *Ordinary Life*. It is very cool and gay.

Thanks to Joy and Kevin for starting [Enter Guild Name Here], from which I borrowed The Coconut Ducks. The guild was important to me during the hardest parts of my childhood.

Thanks again to the Ontario Arts Council for the grant! It's still weird being paid by the government to write!

I lived in Kitchener as a teenager. There are places made up for this book, like The Souper Centre, and places that exist as described, like Mt. Trashmore. The city will always have a place in my heart and it's been lovely writing about it.

I also grew up in Bright before then. I love it in the complicated way one loves family, and my time there was often terrible. While me and my queer friends left town, everywhere was more homophobic in the early 2000s and I hope, like I hope for all places, that Bright has become a more welcoming place to queer folks.

And, of course, thanks to you for reading.

M
MARQUIS
Québec, Canada